I0730797

Victoria's Family
Human, Alien, Hybrid
A Novel

by

Janis A. Pryor

Victoria's Family
Copyright 2021 – Janis A. Pryor
All rights reserved.
Printed in the United States of America

No part of this book may be used or reproduced, stored in a retrieval system, or transmitted in any form or by any means, electronic, mechanical, photocopying, recording, or otherwise, without the prior written permission of the author except in the case of brief quotations embodied in critical articles or reviews.

ISBN – 978-1-949802-23-8

Published by Black Pawn Press

FIRST EDITION

This book is dedicated to the late John Mack, M.D., a dear friend and a brilliant doctor who helped so many of us navigate and integrate the vast territory of extraordinary experiences.

Merriam Webster… Family

The basic unit in society traditionally consisting of two parents rearing their children.

A group of people or peoples deriving from a common stock.

Family: household, kinfolk, relatives, lineage…

PART ONE
Meet Victoria's Family

CHAPTER ONE
Something's Not Right

It was a room a bookworm, intellectual, or writer would love. Two of the four walls, floor to ceiling, were filled with books showing evidence of use. Every book was worn with some pages dog-eared, others full of stickies. The titles of the books ran the gamut from fairy tales to physics. The red, wooden library ladder was always in use.

The third wall was home to a standard sized bed heaped high with blankets, pillows, a puffy down comforter, its mattress dressed in flowered sheets with two stuffed animals. One was a white bunny with soul searching blue eyes, long eyelashes, standing on its hind legs with its paws crossed patiently waiting. Next to the bunny was an ominous owl, white and grey, with wings so realistic you thought it would take off any moment. The owl's eyes were penetrating. They instinctively searched and pinpointed whatever was true for you.

The fourth wall had two large windows that overlooked Riverside Drive, the West Side Highway, and the Hudson River. In front of the windows was an enormous desk, piled high with books, notebooks, papers, a clock radio, and a wide variety of pens and pencils. Right in the middle was Victoria's laptop. Underneath the desk was a wastepaper basket and the legs of a modern desk chair designed to be ergonomically correct. Dangling down from the seat of the chair were two small legs that didn't quite reach the floor. Legs wrapped in blue jeans. Feet covered with red ballet flats and brightly colored red patterned socks.

Seated behind the desk, was a petite twelve-year-old. Her

thick coal black hair was poised on her shoulders, braided with a red ribbon on each braid, red glasses, a grey sweatshirt that was too big for her, and a black turtleneck sweater underneath. Her blue-black eyes could manipulate time in this dimension and delve into the darkest corners of your soul. Yet she was and is the essence of cuteness, her face highlighted by freckles scattered across her nose and cheeks. They danced on the surface of her pale, tan skin making one think she was biracial and magical. Her beautifully shaped fingers were flying across the keyboard. You could feel her concentrating. It was that powerful. You could also sense the peculiar perfection Victoria embodied. That perfection was reflected in an oil portrait that hung next to her bed. It was remarkable for the emotion it captured. It was done by Victoria's best friend at school, Ginger. Ginger is also twelve.

Looking up from her laptop, Victoria sees her bedroom door slightly ajar. Focusing her eyes intently on the door, it slowly closes. This is Victoria, often referred to as Vic by her family.

Victoria wrote in her laptop diary:

My school, the East Side School for Girls, is great! There are only three hundred students there and I am one of ten students of color. It's very fancy. But I really want to go to the Solomon School and make Aunt Sidney and Uncle Stephan proud. They're not my real aunt and uncle but that doesn't matter. I love them. Aunt Sidney is fascinating. It bothers my mother that Aunt Sidney is lighter skinned than she is and doesn't follow the rules. That's because she thinks differently. She's also an artist and does some really amazing paintings. She wears cool clothes too! And Uncle Stephan... he was handsome and smart. My grandmother didn't like him because they were an interracial couple. For a teacher, Gram can be stupid sometimes. Everybody knew how much in love they were. They were always holding hands or had their arms around each other. Uncle Stephan couldn't stop looking at Aunt Sidney sometimes. It was like a movie! Anyway, he had his own company and did important work with the government. Uncle Stephan gave the best hugs in the world. Christopher and I were totally safe when we were with them. We didn't have to worry about anything. I really love him! When they got married, I was a flower girl. I wish they were my parents. Uncle Stephan was murdered because of his work, but I'm not supposed to know that. I miss him. Sometimes Aunt Sidney and I sit quietly and just think about him and hug each other. Our thoughts often blend.

Mom would let Chris and me go with them when they went up to their country place. It's a great house. It's bright and sunny and wonderful, with so many things to look at. That's where Chris and I had that encounter with the owl and the bunny. Chris says he doesn't remember. It was too long ago. Chris is lying. He remembers. Aunt Sidney and Uncle Stephan remembered. They should've been our parents. I feel like Chris and I are living in a mistake. But Chris is not a mistake. He protects me from Dad. Chris is the best big brother anybody could have. We tease each other a lot. I know I can be a smart ass, but he loves me and I love him. I'm his brainy little sister and he's proud of that and a little afraid. And Mom? Really, really intelligent, but we think she's a little crazy. Chris and I discussed it. My mother's a college professor at Columbia University. She teaches Contemporary American Politics. Sometimes she's on TV talking about Congress or the President. I really respect smart people. My mother's brothers are very cool and very smart. Gram is proud of them. Grampa was always bragging about his sons. Uncle David is a brilliant defense attorney and Uncle Kevin is a wealthy investment banker. Just wait until everybody finds out all the things I can do. So far, I've kept almost everything under wraps at home. School is the only place where I can be all of my real self. Sometimes I talk to Ms. Butterfield about all this. She is a very special headmistress and I'm learning a lot from her. She's not afraid of me. But my father, Robert Pittman, asshole extraordinaire, attorney to every jerk on Wall Street, is a problem. He better leave me alone because somebody's coming for him.

Looking over her left shoulder, Victoria says, "I'm right, aren't I? And it's you know who, isn't it?"

A small, spindly looking, beige Alien, ancient in demeanor, with a female presence and big, black eyes, smiles. She touches Victoria's forehead. They smile warmly at each other exchanging messages meant only for the two of them. Victoria puffs up with joy, presses her lips together and smiles while holding her breath. With primordial elegance, the Alien turns, walks through the wall, and disappears.

Excited and pleased Victoria exhales and says out loud, "That is so cool. I've got to learn how to do that."

"Victoria! C'mon, lunch is ready." Catherine, Victoria's mother, had a commanding voice that makes you think she had been in the military! It could send a chill down your back.

Victoria shuts down her laptop and quickly walks into the kitchen with a fierceness and focus most people found unnerving in a twelve-year-old. She sits next to Chris, sixteen and tall for his age. He's at that stage where teenage boys are all legs and arms! At one end of the kitchen island is their father, his head buried in a newspaper. Chris and

Victoria watch him for a minute, look at each other, and roll their eyes.

"Listen, you two. Don't start," Catherine whispers. She places before them a platter of deli sandwiches and a tureen of tomato soup. Bowls, plates and flatware were already placed at each seat. "C'mon, don't dawdle. I want you to be on time for your tutors this afternoon."

Taking two sandwiches and serving himself a bowl of soup, Chris says, "Mom, this business of seeing the tutor on Saturdays sucks."

"Well, young man, that's your fault. B minus in English isn't acceptable in this house."

A heavy silence fell throughout the kitchen. Muffled sounds of traffic swept across the room. All you clearly heard was the sound of silverware being used to eat soup. One sip at a time, a bite of their sandwiches, chewing quickly, no real conversation, the silence was toxic, and then Bob spoke.

"So why is the brainiac going to a tutor?" Bob asks.

"I'm helping my tutor, Dad, and don't talk about me like I'm not here," Victoria said.

"You're helping the tutor… You're twelve. What the hell can you contribute?" Bob glared at his daughter. Catherine glared at Bob and their son glared at both of them.

"Mom, can I be excused? I have some things to do before we leave," Victoria said.

"You're not going to eat the other half of your sandwich?" Chris asked, eyeing the remains of a pastrami sandwich.

Catherine, wide eyed, says, "Chris, you just gobbled down two sandwiches!"

"I'm a growing boy, Mom!" Victoria grins and pushes her

unfinished sandwich towards Chris.

Catherine sighs. You'd think she had the weight of the world on her shoulders. Her world was her family. "Vic, you're excused. You've got a half hour, then it's out the door."

"Thank you. I'll be ready. Chris, you better be ready too."

"Me?! You're the one that's always late, freckle face."

"I am not!" She gives her brother a look, sticks her tongue out at him, and marches to her room. Now it's time for Christopher to grin. The parents are not amused.

A heavy silence returns generated primarily by Bob. He's looking at Chris as if his son came from outer space.

"You still harboring this fantasy about being an architect?" Bob asked his son.

"It's not a fantasy, Dad. There's a reason they admitted me to a studio class in architecture next spring at Columbia," Chris states. "Remember Dad, I'm still in high school!"

"How many black architects you know? How many?" Bob asked. "You can't name one. Why don't…"

Chris cuts in, "That doesn't mean I can't be an architect and there is one I really admire. His name is Adjaye. He's brilliant. Not too long ago the idea of a Black lawyer was a joke."

"You think they're going to let you become an architect? They've got one. They don't want another you. Did you forget you're black?" Bob spit out.

"Impossible in this household," Chris mutters. He finishes his bowl of soup.

"I don't know who or what your sister thinks she is. Maybe she's the one giving you these crazy ideas," Bob said.

Catherine took a deep breath and said, "Bob, do you have to be so hostile, especially to Victoria?"

"She's not right," Bob said.

"Oh, please. She's going to end up in some shrink's office because of you."

"Hmph! That ain't likely. It'll be you and me first. She's a freak and her brother isn't far behind."

"Stop calling her a freak," yelled Chris. "She's just smarter than you, than all of us."

Bob clenches his teeth. He wants to say something but he doesn't. Catherine continues to read her students' papers on her laptop, pretending she's not there.

Straightening out the newspaper, Bob looks at his son and asks, "Why are you still here?"

"I'm finishing lunch. Is that okay?"

"Boy, don't you use that tone of voice with me."

"And what tone of voice is that, Dad?"

Slamming shut her laptop, Catherine glares at them. "Okay, look. Everybody, calm down, right now. Give it a rest. Christopher, get your things ready. Put your dishes in the dishwasher. There's no maid service here."

He stands, takes the dishes, and says, "Yes ma'am." His long legs stop at the dish washer and then take him to his bedroom.

Shaking her head back and forth, Catherine says, "Bob, what is wrong with you? What are you doing to our children?"

"You want to have this conversation?"

"When they leave. They don't need to hear us yelling and screaming at each other." She gets up and walks to Chris' bedroom.

His room is what many teenage boys create. Confusion. It was a mess! Clothes scattered everywhere. His bed unmade but his walls were filled with framed architectural drawings. Books that didn't fit in his bookcases were stacked on the floor. On his nightstand were framed photos, one with his mother somewhere in a rural setting, a group photo with his mother, Victoria, Stephan and Sidney at a restaurant, another with Chris and Victoria taken by Catherine when they were talking to each other unaware of what she was doing. Anyone looking at that photo would know Chris and Victoria adored each other, and were thick as thieves, bonded in a way that transcended the spoken word.

There was a basketball on the floor and his tennis racket was resting on the bed underneath a stack of magazines. His desk was populated with a laptop, two math books, a sketch pad, a worn copy of The Fire Next Time, by James Baldwin, and a container holding various kinds of pencils, rulers, etc. The room felt full of energy. And although it was a mess, Chris knew where everything was.

Catherine knocked on his door that was half opened.

"Hey Mom," Chris said without turning.

"Listen," Catherine said as she walked in and looked around disapprovingly, "What are you wearing? Nothing with a hood."

"I'm wearing my parka and a knitted ski hat!"

"If the police…"

"Mom, I got it. Be polite, don't talk back, do everything they say… I got it," Chris said while putting on his parka. "Make sure they can see both your hands. And don't be a smart ass!"

"Watch over Victoria," Catherine said quietly.

"Watch over Victoria!? She doesn't need watching over. You know what she can do."

Walking over to her son, standing right in front of him, Catherine says, "I don't want to talk about that. Just let it alone and watch over her. Everything will be fine. Okay? This is just some crazy phase she's going through."

"Telekinesis is a phase? That telepathic thing she does, is a phase? If you say so," Chris said. Anything to appease his mother.

Victoria was throwing things into her backpack, her laptop, some snacks, two books and a yellow legal pad. She didn't notice that a third book she needed slid silently to the floor. She zipped up her parka, wrapped her long, knitted scarf around her neck, turned around and found her father standing in the doorway.

"Why don't you knock, Dad? Mom says it's the polite thing to do."

Bob examined his daughter with his eyes. He clenched his teeth before stating, "I saw what you did."

"What are you talking about?" Victoria asked.

"I see how you move things, what you do to plants…and people. You're a witch."

"I'm a witch? People will think you're crazy if you say that out loud. Please move."

Bob stood his ground. Victoria looked into his eyes and he found himself slowly sinking to the floor. His face froze. Her jaw clenched, securing a look of complete defiance and contempt. Once he hit the floor, unable to move, Victoria stepped over him. Chris and her mother were waiting in the hallway. Vic and Chris kissed their mom and left.

Catherine sat down in the living room and continued to read her students' papers. It was cloudy outside. The sun had given up. The sky was pregnant with snow. Maybe they would have a white Thanksgiving this year.

The living room was really an exhibition space with plants and books and sculptures and paintings and magazines galore. Not Vogue or Elle but Foreign Policy, The Economist, and The Atlantic. There were a half dozen photos of Catherine's family. No photos of Bob's family. Resting in front of one of the club chairs was a pile of unread editions of the New Yorker.

"What's wrong with you? Why are you limping?" Catherine asked Bob. His legs seemed wobbly but he made it to a chair.

Bob looked at his wife with a face full of rage. He sat down, and said, "I don't know how much more of Victoria I can take."

"What do you mean?" Catherine took a deep breath and exhaled slowly.

"You know exactly what I mean. Between her and the crap going on at work… Something's got to give."

Catherine closed her laptop and set it on the coffee table. Looking directly at Bob, she said, "Why don't you quit?"

"Quit? And go where?"

"Another firm, Bob!"

"And how are we going to pay for this?" he asked.

"You're not the only making a six-figure salary," Catherine said.

He stood up, tangled with tension. "You would throw that up in my face."

"For God's sake. What do you want from me, Bob? What

am I supposed to do? Just tell me," Catherine said. Bob now loomed over her.

"You're the reason I'm having trouble at work."

Catherine looked up and all she saw was his fist racing to her face. Upon impact, she fell sideways on the couch. Bob grabbed her by the arm and dragged her into the powder room. He pushed her face into the mirror.

"You're an ugly bitch! Look at you! Nobody wants to go to an office party with you. You got the damned braids. What is that?!" He started to shake her by the shoulders.

"Let go of me, Bob. I'm tired of you…"

Before she could finish the sentence, he hit her again and she fell. He pushed her out of the way with his foot and left. Catherine stayed on the floor until she heard Bob slam their bedroom door. She tried to get up and the room started to spin. Leaning against the vanity, she slowly turned and looked in the mirror. Blood dripped from her lower lip onto her blouse. She knew her face would eventually show the bruises. This was one of the few times she was grateful for being dark skinned. Those bruises would scream from your face if you were as light as Sidney, Catherine thought. As soon as the powder room stopped spinning, and she felt steady enough, she tiptoed to the hall closet, got her coat, hat and bag, and left. Waiting for the elevator, she pulled up the collar of her coat, tucked her chin down to hide the split lip, and as much of her face as possible. While waiting for Casey, the doorman, to hail her a cab, Catherine realized she was crying. She didn't notice there was a tall, well-dressed man watching her from across the street. As soon as the cab stopped to pick her up, he vanished.

CHAPTER TWO
Meet Sidney, the Best Friend

Catherine told the driver Sidney's address. Catherine leaned back in the cab and wiped her face with a tissue. It didn't help. Tears fell from her eyes like buckets of dirty water being thrown out a window. The tears raced down her checks to her mouth. The tears were salty.

"I've got to pull myself together," Catherine thought. "Sidney's going to lose her mind when she sees me. I could hear it in her voice when I called. She's going to make me go to that shrink…"

"Lady, we're here," the driver said.

Catherine looked around and realized she had arrived. She glanced at the meter, then pulled out a bill from her wallet, handed it to the driver, and got out. He noticed her hand was shaking.

"Lady, you gave me too much," the driver said. "Way too much."

"Keep it," Catherine muttered.

"You gave me fifty bucks!"

Catherine was already going up the steps to Sidney's brownstone. This elegant home was famous among Sidney's friends. Stephan gave it to her as a wedding present. They had four fairytale years together before the accident.

Catherine knocked on the door thinking, "A fairy-tale is possible when you're filthy rich and your husband's not only gorgeous and kind, but brilliant and white also. Damn." Before she could knock again, Catherine heard the familiar barking of Bonwit and Coco, Sidney's cocker-spaniels, the most pampered and well cared for spaniels on the east coast. Catherine was convinced they were really people disguised as dogs!

The door opened with Sidney holding onto the spaniels. "Come on in," Sidney said and closed the door behind Catherine. "You sounded awful on the phone. What's wrong?"

Catherine, standing with her back to Sidney, took off her coat only to feel Sidney's hand on her shoulder. Catherine dropped her head as Sidney gently turned her around. More tears creeped down Catherine's face.

"Oh my God, Catherine," Sidney said as she looked at Catherine's face. "Come on." Sidney led Catherine to the living room and sat her down. The spaniels were already there sitting in Sidney's favorite chair. "He's going to kill you one day, if this keeps up. Where's Christopher and Victoria? Did they see this? Where are they? You didn't leave them there with him not after last week, did you?"

Slowly Catherine looked up at her and said, "No. They've gone to their tutors." Catherine couldn't help but notice how much Sidney looked like Victoria. They were both petite, light-skinned, black hair and dark eyes, and both had these freckles scattered across their noses and cheeks. For some reason the freckles were more unnerving to Catherine than anything else.

"Stay right here. I'm going down to the kitchen to get some ice. Coco and Bonwit are going to watch you, so don't try anything."

Catherine managed to laugh. "I'm not going anywhere." She leaned back on the couch and slowly looked around. Catherine had been in this room a thousand times. The house was still filled with love, with admiration, passion, affection and respect. It never ceased to amaze her, the beauty and peacefulness that Sidney's and Stephan's homes had. It was palpable. Catherine was convinced something mystical went on in this house and whatever it was, it had intensified since Stephan died almost a year ago. All the things Sidney and Stephan felt for each other, Catherine had never known with Bob.

Catherine didn't give much credence to spirituality and New Age thinking, but she found herself wondering if Sidney's house had some kind of aura around it, if Stephan's spirit was still here.

Sidney raced up the stairs with some ice cubes wrapped in paper towels and handed it to Catherine. "What happened this time?"

Catherine shrugged her shoulders and pressed the ice against the side of her face. "I don't know, Sidney. He's under a lot of pressure. Ever since he made partner, he's...different."

"Different? No. He's crazy and you're not going back there tonight."

"Sidney, I can't stay here..." Catherine noticed Sid had a funny look on her face. It was as if she was watching something no one else could see. "Sidney?"

"We've got to go back to your condo, right now, before Chris and Vic get back. C'mon. Get up. Put your coat on."

Confused, her head throbbing with pain, Catherine looked at Sidney, "What? You do this stuff."

"Listen to me. Your children are going to need you. Now c'mon. My car's right outside."

"It always is..."

CHAPTER THREE
Vic & Chris

Chris and Vic were standing on the corner of Broadway and 82nd waiting for the light to change. It was getting dark already and cold. Regardless of what the calendar said, fall was over. Victoria was looking through her backpack, listening to Chris with one ear.

"Vic, don't mess with the streetlights. You caused a traffic jam last time you did that."

"I forgot my other math book. We have to go back."

"You forgot? We're going to be late, Vic. If we hadn't stopped to get pizza…! Mom's going to be mad. Do we really have to go back?"

"I'm sorry," she said. "But yes, we have to go back. There're some mistakes in my math book that I have to show her."

Christopher sighs, throws up his hands, and turns around to head back to their building. "I can hear it now," Chris says to no one in particular. West End Avenue wasn't that far away. Towering over his sister, he puts his hands on her shoulders thinking that would make her walk quicker, but it didn't.

"Christopher, I'm fine. I don't need you to guide me down the street. We'll be there in a minute or two."

"Okay, okay…" Christopher said.

They continued to walk and Victoria stopped. Chris stopped and looked at her. She had turned to look at him. "You know I love you, right?"

He squints at his little sister and puts his hands on her shoulders again. She looks up, wide open face, big eyes that were oddly serious right now.

"You know I love you, right?" she repeated with complete seriousness.

Stunned, he said, "What are you talking about?"

"I'm not going to be around much longer, but nothing's going to happen to you. I'll make sure of that. But if something bad does happen, it won't matter where I am. I'll come fix it. I'll always make sure you're safe. If I need to, I'll come get you. You protected me. I'll protect you, okay?"

Dumbstruck, Chris says, "Okay." He realizes they're standing in the middle of the sidewalk with people walking around them. "C'mon freckle face. Let's go find your book." They walked in silence for a few minutes when he turned to her and said, "What do you want me to say?"

"Nothing, you just need to know."

CHAPTER FOUR
Things Children Should Not See

Victoria and Christopher turned the corner and walked to their building. Victoria, focused as always with Christopher just a few steps behind her. Casey, their doorman, smiles as they approach.

"Did we forget something?" he asks.

Victoria looks annoyed and shoots a look at him that made Casey flinch a little. He looks at Chris for confirmation of something, anything. Casey adored Victoria but she was a unique piece of work for a twelve-year-old. She would always be a unique piece of work, regardless of age.

Chris turns toward Casey and states, "Of course."

They head to the elevator and wait while Casey begins to remember. He froze. What could he say? What could he do to delay the kids from going up to their unit? Small, explosions went off inside of him, ignited by panic. The elevator door opened and Chris and Vic stepped in, turned and waved at Casey. He gave them a limp wave back, closed his eyes and muttered to himself, "Oh God…"

Casey goes back to his post at the door. Stands stiff as a tree while inside his brain thoughts run amuck. "What the hell is the matter with people? Goddamn Mr. Pittman. He's a fool. Such a nice lady for a wife, two beautiful kids, and what does he do? He's a cheap bastard too." Casey was snatched from his thoughts as he saw Catherine and Sidney pull up and begin to park right in front of the building. It was as if the space was waiting for her.

"Listen, Miss Psychic," Catherine said. "You want to tell me why we're doing this?"

"All I know, is you've got to be here." Sidney turned off the ignition, grabbed her bag and said, "C'mon."

Sidney got out of her SUV, nimble as a cat. Catherine reluctantly follows. Sidney smiles at Casey and nods her head as she flies by. Sidney had grown up in this neighborhood. She knew most of the doormen in the surrounding area. Casey had watched Sidney walk a succession of cocker spaniels for close to thirty years. He had observed that she had an uncanny way of keeping her spaniels healthy and long living. Every now and then he jokingly thought that it would be great to come back in another life as one of Sidney's spaniels!

Catherine drags along after Sidney forgetting about what she looked like until she saw the look on Casey's face. The elevator was on the top floor. It would take some time for it to come back down to the lobby. It was all Sidney could do not to scream.

Chris unlocks the door to their condo. Victoria marches into the living room, surveying every nook and corner when Chris grabs her. He motions for her to be quiet and whispers, "Get behind me." He picks up a vase from a nearby table. "Listen," he whispers. Victoria got in front of him instead.

Muffled voices, interspersed with gasping and moaning sounds come from the direction of the bedrooms. Christopher panics and reaches for Victoria, but she's just out of his reach. They follow the noise to their parent's bedroom. The moans and now laughter, were louder. Chris was afraid he and Victoria would find their parents kissing or worse. He and some of his friends had watched some porn online. The sounds coming from his parents' bedroom were very similar to the sounds he and his friends heard when they watched two people having sex.

"Vic, get back here," Christopher ordered. She paid no attention to him.

The bedroom door was slightly ajar. Vic carefully pushed it open. Christopher set the vase next to the bedroom door. Victoria sees a naked, white back with shoulder length blonde hair, on top of her father bouncing up and down. Her father was moaning and grunting.

Christopher mutters, "Oh God…" He reached for Victoria and something stopped him and his arm dropped. It felt like his hand hit an invisible wall.

Victoria was still trying to comprehend what she was seeing. She thought, "I don't think this should be happening…" She focused her eyes on the bed. Within seconds the bed was rising. Her father and the blonde woman were oblivious to everything. Then, in what felt like a nano second, the bed flipped over.

"Holy shit," Christopher muttered.

Their father had fallen out of bed, shocked. He grabbed the sheet and tried to wrap it around him. The blonde woman started to sputter and scream. She looked around and found herself on the floor. Reaching for the spread, she covered her body. When she looked up, she found two black eyes that seemed to be the source of physical pain that almost paralyzed her body for a few seconds. When the pain subsided, she realized that Victoria was the source of it. The paralytic pain came from Vic's eyes. The blonde woman crawled to the bathroom and slammed the door.

Bob found his pants and was hurriedly putting them on,

swearing at his son. Victoria heard him. She turned and looked at him with the kind of stillness you associated with horror movies.

"Vic! Vic!" Chris said. Victoria heard nothing.

Bob takes a step towards his daughter. That's all he could do. He found himself paralyzed, face to face with his daughter's eyes. He didn't understand how she was doing all this. All he saw were her black eyes. The longer he looked into her eyes the more he felt as if he were drowning. He took a half breath and started to scream like a crescendo passage in music. It was a scream that came from his soul. It was deep and unnaturally long. The sound registered through every cell in his body. Chris was witness to this demonstration of his sister's mysterious power while his father was bellowing in pain, begging Victoria to stop.

At that moment, Sidney and Catherine walked in the condo and heard Bob. Sidney flies down the hall followed by Catherine. The young blonde-haired woman races by them, now fully dressed and red-faced, desperately hoping no one recognized her. Chaos ensued.

Catherine was overwhelmed, vacillating between rage and heartbreak. Christopher tried to watch everybody. His father stopped screaming and collapsed to the floor. With all the pain savaging his body, he still managed to have that look in his eye that said, "Somebody's going to pay for this."

And Sidney? Her face was absolutely still also. Her eyes were fixated on Bob but she went directly to Victoria and held her. She seemed to be in shock, her eyes robotically blinking. Bob balled up his fist and stepped towards her. Christopher stepped between them and knocked his father flat on his behind.

"Oh, my God! Christopher, what have you done?" Catherine asked. She was trying not to shake.

"What I always do, stand between my jerk ass father and my sister." Victoria was now quietly gasping for breath.

"Christopher, please..." Catherine didn't know what to do. Her husband had been knocked out by their son. And their daughter was in shock, or something, and Sidney? Sidney would take care of everything.

"Listen," Sidney said. "All of you go pack some things. We're going to my house. Get your clothes, your books, whatever you can grab. Your father and I are going to have a conversation. Go." Sidney hugged Victoria. "Catherine, you too. Go. None of you are staying here anymore."

Catherine took a deep breath and said, "Okay. C'mon kids, let's get our things. C'mon. Now." They followed their mother leaving Sidney and Bob alone.

Bob was still sprawled on the floor, rubbing his jaw. He tried to avoid Sidney's eyes but couldn't. She squatted down and said, "You're done." Bob starts to say something but she interrupts him with, "Don't."

"One day, you and I are..."

"Are what? You better pray Chris and Victoria don't tell me all you've done. And don't think I haven't heard how you lock Victoria in the closet. I am on to you."

CHAPTER FIVE
Sidney's Brownstone

Everybody trudges in with overnight bags, back packs, tote bags, dropping them in the hallway. Bonwit and Coco sniff everything and everyone. In one arm, Victoria clutches Mr. Bunny, in the other, Misty, the stuffed owl with yellow eyes.

"C'mon," Sidney said. "Let's all go downstairs to the kitchen." Sidney puts on a kettle of water and everybody else sits around the kitchen island. A relieved silence sets in. Victoria watches Sidney and puts Misty, the owl, and Mr. Bunny on the stool next to her. Both had extraordinary eyes.

Victoria takes a deep look at her mother as if she was walking through Catherine's soul. Christopher's knuckles are bruised and slightly swollen. He's lightly tapping the fingers on his right hand with the speed of light, biting his lower lip. Catherine's staring into space.

"I don't ever want to go back to the condo, Mom. Dad's crazy and he scares me."

"Baby, please. I'm sorry you had to see that. I'm sorry both of you had to see your father like that." She stopped, still lost in despair. "You know, I need a glass of wine."

"What do we do about Mr. Solomon?" Victoria asked.

"Who's Mr. Solomon?" Sidney asked.

"Vic thinks he's God," Chris said.

"Be quiet. He's not God," Victoria said and frowned at her brother.

Sighing, Catherine said, "He runs this special school. Ms. Butterfield, the headmistress at Vic's school, thinks Victoria should go there. Bob and I are supposed to meet Mr. Solomon next week."

"What's the name of the school?" Sidney asked.

"The Solomon School for Girls," Catherine said. She got up and said, "I've got to call your tutors. They probably think you were abducted or run over in traffic. Gotta get my cell. I'll be right back." Holding tightly onto the rail, Catherine carefully walks up the stairs.

Right behind her a small, beige Alien follows her up the stairs. The Alien is visible only to Victoria and Sidney. They look at each other, showing nothing that would indicate they saw this creature creeping up the stairs behind Catherine. But they both knew. Victoria exhales. Sidney gives her a reassuring look.

"Hey, what's going on?" Chris asks.

"Nothing," Sidney said. "If you sense anything, it's probably stress." Sidney got some mugs from the cabinet, opened the freezer and pulled out a pint of gourmet, vanilla ice cream.

"I don't think so. It's something strange," Christopher said quietly. Sidney avoided looking at him. Christopher looks around the kitchen and into the dining room. He looks at Vic for some sign…of anything…but nothing. Christopher loudly sighs. "Are you going to make your special latte?" Chris asked.

"Yeah, I thought I'd fix some for all of us."

Beaming, Victoria asks, "Like what Uncle Stephan used to fix me when you were out?"

"Yup. He told me you liked it."

"It was great! I miss him," Victoria said.

"I know you do," Sidney said. "I miss him too."

"I know," Victoria said.

"He was a cool dude," Christopher said.

Victoria walks over to a slightly drooping plant at the end of the island. She puts her hands around the plant, barely touching the leaves. The plant revives. Chris, watching her, rolls his eyes and shakes his head.

"What are you staring at, Chris?" Victoria asks with a satisfied smile on her face.

"Nothing," Chris says and looks at Sidney who's trying to hide her smile. "What's taking Mom so long?"

"I'll bet she's rescheduling," Sidney said. She puts three scoops of vanilla ice cream in a small stainless steel bowl. Victoria watches intently.

"Wow," whispers Christopher. "I didn't know you put ice cream in it."

A low-key buzzing sound begins to fill the air, barely audible but distinct. Chris sits up straight and looks around. "What is that?" he asks.

Victoria walks over to the kitchen window and looks out.

Sidney watches her.

"Aunt Sidney, what is that? Where's that noise coming from?"

"It happens sometimes, Chris. It comes and goes. Look, tell me how long your father has been having these outbursts."

Victoria is fixated at the window. There's a small beam of light falling from the sky into Sidney's backyard. The light fades.

"Dad's been crazy ever since Victoria started talking! He keeps telling this story about how Victoria never cried when she was born." Chris turns and looks at Victoria who's still peering out the window. "Hey freckle face, what are you looking at?"

Victoria sits back down at the kitchen island and says, "Nothing."

"Right," Chris said sarcastically.

"That's what your father talks about?" Sidney asked perplexed.

"Yeah. He's been slightly nuts ever since. And it's gotten worse since he was promoted to partner."

"Why didn't you say something about your father's outbursts?"

Chris and Vic said in unison, "Mom would kill us!"

"Okay, I got it. I knew your mom and dad were having some problems but I didn't think it was quite this bad. So...Christopher, when you brought Victoria over here because she'd had a fight with Bob... There was more to it than that, wasn't it?" Sidney paused to pour powdered chai in their mugs followed by some boiling water to dissolve the powder.

Christopher let out a heavy sigh while Vic looked at him and then Sidney.

"Well, yeah Aunt Sidney. I had to get her out of there. It wasn't safe. Dad's got this thing about Vic. It's crazy."

Sidney stared at them for what felt like days and days. Victoria started to fidget in her seat.

"Listen, both of you can always come over here when things get out of hand. I'll give you a key. You understand? Just like you and Vic did. You don't have to call." Sidney stirs the mix in their cups.

They nodded their heads.

"But I'm never going back to the condo, Aunt Sidney," Victoria stated with authority.

"You can stay here as long as you like," Sidney said.

Victoria's face beamed with a sense of security.

"Okay, tell me about this school." She motioned for Sid and Chris to take a sip of their latte before she delivered the crowning touch.

"It's really special. Mr. Solomon comes once a year to see if there're any students smart enough to attend. I think, my friend, Ginger and I are being considered because he's been back to talk to us a lot."

"That's all she talks about, Aunt Sidney, for weeks! Charles Solomon! You'd think he was the second coming." Christopher turns and grins at Victoria. He's getting ready to tease her. "I think you've got a crush on him!"

"Nobody asked you! Stop talking!"

"Well somebody's got to take you on," Chris said and straightened his shoulders.

Victoria sticks her tongue out at him and says loudly, "It doesn't have to be you!"

Sidney is trying to hide her amusement as she puts a scoop of softened vanilla ice cream in each one of their mugs. She takes a small beater and begins to whip the contents in every cup so it's thicker and foamy. Catherine walks down the stairs with Coco and Bonwit watching her.

"Why does your house look like it should be in a magazine, and my house looks like mid-century Good Will?" Catherine walks over to the window and looks out and up for a moment. She sits down next to Christopher but looks one more time out the window. "Did y'all see that light outside a minute or two ago?"

Sidney quietly said, "Yeah, we noticed it."

"Well, where did it come from?" Catherine asked, perplexed and frustrated.

"It came from the sky, Mom," Victoria said.

"Sometimes, little girl, you can be too cute."

Christopher intercedes and says, "We're talking about Charles Solomon, Victoria's boyfriend."

"Stop it, Chris. He's not my boyfriend. He's very intelligent," Victoria said with a frown on her face. "You just wait, Chris. You'll meet him and then you'll see."

Catherine takes Christopher's hand and kisses it. She exhales and looks at everybody before continuing. "Look, I don't know if your father is going to meet Mr. Solomon. Your father has issues."

"When do you have to meet with him?" Sidney asked.

"I'll check my calendar for the exact date," Catherine said. "But it's sometime next week."

"Bob will be there. I'll give him a call," Sidney said.

"Whoa," Christopher said softly.

"Aunt Sidney, can you fix mom's face in time to meet Mr.

Solomon?" Victoria asked. "She should look her best." Victoria licked the thick vanilla chai latte off of her spoon. She put it back in her mug. Her eyes were staring beyond Sidney for a moment and then she looked at her mother. "I think Christopher and I should make sure Mom never gets hurt again. That's why Dad has to die for hurting us."

"Victoria!" Catherine exclaimed! "No!"

"Victoria, who would punish your father? Do you think he should go to jail and die there? Is that what you're saying? Life imprisonment?" Sidney asked.

Victoria thought for a moment and then looked at Sidney, "Go to jail...no. Someone should kill him, Aunt Sidney."

"Do you really know what that means to kill someone?" Sidney asked while looking at Victoria.

Letting out a loud sigh, Victoria replied, "I know what that means. The person never comes back here as a physical person. They're gone and the person who does the killing, they never forget," Victoria said and made a sweeping movement with her right arm to emphasize the point. "Uncle Stephan's dead. I know what that is."

Looking into her own cup of latte, Sidney said, "You know, there's this...idea that the punishment should fit the crime. Do you know what that means?"

"Sort of, if you do something really bad then the punishment should be really bad and if you do something not so bad, you shouldn't be punished so bad. Yes? Like an eye for an eye. That's what Gram says. Mr. Solomon talks about crime and punishment with us."

Catherine was stunned by her daughter's statements.

"Okay, but it doesn't always work. We strive for that

but..." Sidney said.

Victoria cut Sidney off and said, "What my father did was bad, very bad."

"So, he should die?" Sidney asked.

"Aunt Sidney, yes!" Victoria pounded her little fists on the kitchen island to emphasize her point and then looked right at Sidney, confident and calm.

"Don't you think that's a little harsh not to mention illegal?" Sidney asked. "I don't think there's a law in this country that says you have to die for hurting your family... unless you kill them."

"I don't care," Victoria stated, her eyebrows tightening. "Aunt Sidney, he really hurt us. He hurt me. I would feel better if he wasn't here anymore." Victoria pounded her two small fists again on the counter, twice, to emphasize her point. Sidney ignored Catherine whose face was a mask of horror! She couldn't believe what her daughter was saying. Christopher always thought his little sister was not to be toyed with, much less angered. He looked at his folded hands because he didn't know what else to do.

"Is there anymore latte and whipped ice cream? Aunt Sidney, I love this! It so reminds me of Uncle Stephan. Uncle Stephan never hurt you, did he? I mean the way Mom was hurt. I bet he never made fun of you, or embarrassed you, or called you bad names. He never hit you, did he?"

"No. He never did any of those things," Sidney said quietly.

Catherine squirmed in her seat. Christopher watched his mother, expecting the worst, even though he didn't know what the worst would be.

"Okay – listen, about this meeting with Mr. Solomon. Vic,

everybody will look their best," Sidney said. "Tell me what Mr. Solomon talks about with you?"

"Many things! We talk about poverty, war, justice, morals, the environment, and why people do the things they do." Victoria paused, and then said, "See, justice, that's why Dad has to die. It would be justice for Mom."

Catherine and Christopher give Victoria a long look. Sidney is perfectly at ease but never takes her eyes off Victoria. Catherine gets up and walks into the dining room looking for an opened bottle of wine. She returns with white wine and sets it down on the kitchen island in front of her seat.

Sidney asked, "Tell me why you like Mr. Solomon. Those are impressive and important things you two talk about. So, tell me why you like him."

"He doesn't lie, and he's not afraid of smart women." Victoria turned so she directly faced her mother. Vic's eyes narrowed slightly and she let loose in her special way. "Look, Dad always has issues because he has an inferiority complex and he's insecure. He's afraid of smart women too. That's why he hurts you, Mom. And he doesn't like Aunt Sidney either. I make him totally crazy. That's why I have to go to Mr. Solomon's school before Dad does something stupid. There're no guarantees though."

Christopher's mouth was slightly open. Sidney smiled and said to herself, "That's my girl."

Catherine looked at Victoria with incredulity and asked, "Where did you get that from? How do you know these things at twelve?"

"I just do," Victoria said and finished drinking her latte.

CHAPTER SIX
The Brothers-The Uncles-The Protectors

And there they are, walking through the doors of Robert Pittman's law firm, Victoria's favorite uncles, two of the most magnificent men you ever saw. They are elegant, dignified. Their clothing fits perfectly with a timeless sense of style, chic but not garish. They reek quality as a subtle fragrance of after shave envelops their entrance like a summer breeze. The shorter one, David Stockard, walks with such confidence it takes your breath away. His gaze is both chilling and engaging. The taller one, Kevin Stockard, muscular, refined, with the physical command of an athlete and the air of a scholar, looks like he stepped off the pages of a leading men's fashion magazine. Heads held high their brown skin is perfection. Together their stride is both rhythmic and complementary.

It's true, when black men walk it's an event, unless you're Robert Pittman, Victoria's father, and then your walk is a lie.

CHAPTER SEVEN
The Brothers Talk

The shorter one walked over to the receptionist and said, "Good afternoon. My name is David Stockard, and this is my brother, Kevin Stockard. We're here to see Robert Pittman." David watched every move the receptionist made. She was young and barely breathing when she looked at them. Her hair was limp. Her gaze wide eyed. Her skin paler than alabaster.

Looking first at David and then Kevin, she said, "Is he expecting you?"

David said, "I doubt that. This is a personal matter, a family matter that came up suddenly. Is he in?"

A little flustered, she stated, "Well…I'm sure he is but…"

Kevin cut her off and said, "Perhaps you didn't hear what my brother said. This is a family matter of some urgency." Kevin was an imposing man, over six feet tall, and he carried it well. "If I remember, his office is at the end of this hallway," Kevin said while pointing to the area behind the receptionist.

"It is, but I can't let you go back there unless he says so. I'm sorry," the receptionist said while tapping her fingernails gently against the desktop while her right knee bopped up and down underneath the desk faster than a hummingbird's wings.

David focused his eyes on hers. "I understand you have a job to do – so if he gives you any grief, tell him to talk to us, okay? Tell him we didn't give you a choice."

Kevin started walking down the hall. David smiled at the

receptionist and followed Kevin. The receptionist's face stiffened. According to gossip, Bob Pittman could be an unforgiving boss especially since he made partner. The receptionist knew the stories about Bob Pittman Before (he made partner) and Bob Pittman After (he made partner.) He made her skin crawl. As she watched Kevin and David walk away, she closed her eyes for a moment and prayed that she wouldn't get in trouble. Flinging her long, limp, blonde hair out of her face she suddenly reached down and grabbed her bag. It was time to go home! Swallowing hard, she threw her coat on and raced out of the office. She did not want to confront Bob Pittman and she certainly didn't need his wrath.

Kevin and David strode down the hall towards Bob's office. Kevin pointed to five large black and white photos of each partner in the firm. Bob's photo was not among them but there was an empty space for another photo. Kevin thought that maybe that was where Bob's photo was supposed to go. As Kevin and David walked into Bob's office, they looked at each other and slightly shook their heads back and forth.

David asked, "So where's the photo of Bob? You think they forgot to put it up there? I'm just askin'…"

Kevin quietly said, "They don't want his picture up there scaring away potential clients. You can tell by the receptionist's reaction to us, they don't have a lot of black people coming in here. If she tapped her fingers any faster…"

David shook his head and looked at his brother. "You know what Bryan Stevenson said? Slavery hasn't ended. It's just evolved. Bob proves that every day."

Kevin smiled sadly as they stood in Bob's office. It's a dull collection of tasteful, predictable furniture, nothing original, and nothing extreme. His office reminded Kevin of a little ol' lady, wearing a black sheath dress with a double strand of pearls grabbing her neck. Strolling over to Bob's desk, Kevin saw a photo of his sister, Catherine, with Bob. Kevin picked it up and showed it to David who just rolled his eyes. Kevin stopped for a moment and looked at a photo of Bob with Stephan. Kevin studied it for a moment. Stephan and Bob were talking. Bob's smile looked a little forced.

"I still can't believe Stephan's dead. He was a good friend to Bob and Catherine," Kevin said and sighed.

"More like an angel. That was quite a funeral. I don't think Sidney will ever get over it. The look in her eyes... We've known her since forever, and I've never seen her so stricken. You think you've got problems...," David said as he looked around Bob's office.

"I know. Did you see how Stephan's family closed ranks around her at the funeral? Whoa. She won't have to worry about a damned thing."

"Yeah...Sidney's an original. The two of them made a great couple, unlike our sister and this fool." David looked at his watch and wondered how long Bob was going to take.

Putting the photo back, Kevin slowly walked around his brother-in-law's desk while massaging his hands, each one taking turns softening the muscles of the other, bending the fingers, rubbing the palms together. On the wall behind the desk were Bob's degrees, an undergraduate degree from City College and a degree from Columbia University Law School. Staring at the law degree, Kevin flicked his fingers against the glass frame.

"That pisses me off every time I look at it," Kevin said.

Seated on the leather couch opposite Bob's desk, David said, "I know what you mean. Catherine helped put that fool through law school. Dad begged her not to do it." David paused for a moment and then asked, "You think brother Bob has any idea we were coming to see him?"

"No. Who would know to tell him? Cath doesn't know. Mom suspects." David started looking through the New York Times that was on the end table and said, "Thank-God Sidney called me. I loved the way she started the conversation. 'David, if you don't do something about Bob, I will.' " David paused. "She had that tone in her voice... You don't want to mess with her when she sounds like that."

"I know. And then Mom told us what she had seen..." Kevin clenched his jaw and continued with, "Connecting the dots was pretty easy," Kevin said. "But if Sidney hadn't called you..."

"Yup...we should have Sid up to the house..." David said. "We need to do something for her. Stephan stuck his neck out for Bob and Catherine. Stephan walked his talk."

Kevin walked over to the couch, sat down next to David, crossed his legs and said, "A rich man too. Remember what Mom said? 'He was a good white man.' " They chuckled.

"Mom's been talking about going back to Georgia. She's lonely without Dad," David said.

"I know. I gotta tell you, the whole idea makes me nervous," Kevin said.

"I know." Looking at his watch again, David asked Kevin, "You don't think that Negro slipped out, do you?"

"No, his coat and everything's still here."

"Kev, did you finally tell Mom? C'mon man! Sooner or later… I think she already knows. She's just waiting for you to tell her." David said. "She'll flip out and start quoting the Bible, but she'll be okay. Better do it before Thanksgiving."

Kevin looked at his brother, "You're right. But we've gotta deal with this fool right now. I'm losing my patience."

The longer David and Kevin waited the more restless they became. David got up, took Bob's coat and sat back down next to Kevin who then got up and started to slowly pace massaging his hands again.

David held Bob's camel haired coat and slowly examined it. Cashmere. "I want to be ready when that fool gets here. We're wasting no time," David said.

Kevin studied another collection of photos over the couch. The largest photo was in the middle. It was taken the day Bob made partner. He was smiling surrounded by colleagues, his fellow partners, and the founder of the firm, Brendan Collins, a Wall Street legend. Kevin knew Bob had been passed over for partner several times because he was just good and not great. Kevin stuffed his hands in his pants' pockets while looking at another photo of Bob, Catherine, Stephan, and the Mayor at some event. Stephan had his arm around Catherine's waist standing between her and Bob.

Kevin looked at David and said, "He's been here how long, and is still the only black partner, and just one of four African American lawyers on a staff of almost a hundred? There's something wrong with that, man, and his photo isn't up on the wall outside? I mean, c'mon…"

"Yeah. I don't know why he hasn't left," David said. "There're other firms that could use his expertise in corporate law, mergers and acquisitions, taxes. We never have enough tax lawyers. But where else is he gonna make partner? He's a good lawyer, nothing exceptional. We gotta be great before they accept us. You know that. No place for average Negroes in their world. Twice as good to get half as much…"

Kevin said quietly, "Yeah, well Bob's not great. Never has been. He's an average black man in America, making a ton of money just like so many average white men."

"Kev, c'mon. Every day is a struggle for all of us. You don't dare make a mistake, and Bob sure as hell can't afford to make a mistake. Everything's just a little beyond his reach. And this firm? It's known as the snake pit. They'll eat you alive just for fun."

David paused for a moment. "Bob got caught up in this trick bag of success. He ain't ready. Never was ready, and never gon' be ready. You, me, and Cath? We were ready. Mom and Pop made sure of that. Bob didn't have a Mom and Pop. All he had was a junkie for a mother. Excuse me, in today's parlance, 'an addict.' Grew up in some damned project; poor black boy makes good. It's textbook, classic. Bob is the kind of black man that white folks like to show off. Parade 'em around like monkeys in a circus."

"Yeah, well that's a problem not an excuse," Kevin said and sat back down.

Loosening his tie as he walked into his office, Bob's eyes popped seeing both of his brothers-in-law. It was now after six.

"Hey," Bob said! "What are you doing here? Why didn't you call?"

David stood up and said, "If we called, you wouldn't be

here, Bob."

Bob walked over to the couch. As he approached, Kevin stood up. Bob, on a good day, stretched to five foot ten. He stepped back a little to look up at Kevin. As Kevin looked down at Bob, Kevin extended his hand, grabbed Bob's and squeezed it, the same way you would squeeze a lemon or an orange to loosen up the juice.

Bob said, "Hey man. Good to see you." Kevin all but crushed Bob's hand giving him a slow, thorough handshake. "What's up?" Bob asked and winced from the pain in his hand that was now completely covered by Kevin's hand.

"What's up?" David repeated and looked at his brother. "He wants to know what's up?" Looking back at Bob, David said, "Catherine, our sister, that's what's up. Put your coat on and get yourself together. We need to have a little talk." David threw Bob's coat at him.

Startled, Bob jerked and barely caught his coat while saying, "I don't know what Catherine told you but... We've been having some problems and I know how close you all are...but..."

David cut him off. "Cath didn't tell us anything. We haven't talked to her in over a week, have we Kevin?" David was lying but he didn't care at the moment. He was protecting Catherine.

"Nope." Kevin never took his eyes off Bob.

Bob was straining to hear them. The ambient noises of the office clearing out for the day seemed louder than usual. Bob's eyes darted from Kevin to David.

"Button up your coat, Bob. This isn't about what Catherine told us. This is about what our mother saw, the bruises on Catherine. And then Mom told us about that little incident at the condo that drove Cath and the kids to stay with Sid until this is resolved in some way."

"Your mother got it wrong," Bob said and he started to shake his head from side to side and rubbed the back of his neck. It was that quiet tone of his brother-in-law's voices that worried Bob. Then he thought he heard someone walking down the hall.

Kevin walked over to Bob, stepped behind him, and whispered, "You calling our mother a liar?" He placed his hands on Bob's shoulders and then helped him with his coat.

Bob sighed and said, "No…man I'm not saying that." He felt his stomach tighten.

Still standing behind him, Kevin continued with, "Then what are you saying?"

Someone knocked on Bob's office door and they all stopped talking. Standing in the opened door was an older man, white silky hair, weathered skin, crisp blue eyes, well dressed, his eyes examining every one of them. "Bob?"

"Come in, come in." Looking at Kevin and David, Bob said, "I want you to meet the founding partner of the firm, Brendan Collins."

David walked over to him, extended his hand and said, "Pleasure to meet you."

Collins grabbed David's hand, shook it and said, "You're David Stockard, the defense attorney. The newspapers can't photograph you enough. You practice here and D.C. I've been following your career over the years. Would love to have lunch with you one day."

"It would be my pleasure, Mr. Collins," David said while Bob clenched his jaw.

"Brendan. No need for such formality. Call my office,

David. Really, no b.s. – I'd really like to talk with you."

"Oh, by the way….Brendan, what happened to Bob's photo out there? Why is his photo missing from the line-up of partners?"

Brendan turned and looked out at the hallway where the photos were displayed. "Oh… what happened… The glass became cracked somehow. We sent it out to be replaced."

David paused and said, "A-huh. Okay…"

Brendan turned back and scrutinized Kevin. "You played quarterback at Harvard when you were there. I heard you got an offer from the NFL. Surprised you didn't take it." Brendan Collins gazed at Kevin, inspecting every inch of him the way a butcher assesses a side of beef before cutting it up for sale.

Kevin smiled and said, "Playing pro football is akin to being in a car accident every week. You get hurt in ways you don't even notice until it's too late and then there's nothing they can do for you. Thought I'd have a better shot at long term success and a long life going to the Harvard Business School. Fast money is not necessarily smart money."

"Very intelligent man," Brendan said. "Didn't I read a piece about you a few weeks ago in the Wall Street Journal? You brokered a huge deal with the Chinese."

Kevin thought, "Brendan Collins is definitely not to be underestimated." And said, "That would be right."

His eyes still focused on Kevin, Brendan smiled and added, "There was a column in the Amsterdam News also about you."

Kevin and David glanced quickly at each other. David asked, "Mr. Collins, you read the Amsterdam News?"

"Well, it's one of the leading black newspapers in the

country. I like keeping up on you people," he said.

"Well, how about that? Good for you…" David said trying not to glare at Collins.

"Well…I guess the most important thing is that you're Catherine's brothers! She talks about you two every chance she gets whenever I see her, which is not often enough!" Brendan looked right into Bob's eyes. "She's an amazing woman, so very articulate! I saw her last week on some Cable news program commenting on the elections. It was just amazing!"

Bob was barely breathing and for several seconds, nobody said a word. The only thing you could heard was the clock ticking on Bob's desk. The three men were staring at Bob.

Brendan, sensing he was intruding said, "Look, Bob I can see you're busy and this can wait. We can talk in the morning. Good meeting both of you," Brendan said and walked out with a slight limp that David noticed.

When Collins was out of ear shot, David looked at his brother and said, "…you people….damn."

Staring at the floor, all Kevin said was, "Hmph…it never changes. And Catherine is 'articulate" as if it's a miracle she can speak the English language."

"How did he get that limp?" David asked.

Bob quietly said, "He was injured in college playing football. He almost lost the leg."

Kevin asked, "Did he go to Harvard?"

Bob glared at Kevin and said, "Class of '69."

Kevin met his brother-in-law's gaze and said, "I'd sure hate for you to get injured. Come on. Let's go."

"I've got work to do this evening," Bob mumbled.

David turned and looked at him. "Not tonight, my brother. Not tonight."

CHAPTER EIGHT
The Men Talk

An anonymous, black, Lincoln Town Car was waiting for them as they stepped out of the building and onto the sidewalk. There was a chill in the air, more than appropriate for mid-November in New York City. The clocks had been turned back a week or so ago. By 4:30 in the afternoon it was getting dark outside. The red, yellow and green lights looked like shiny gumdrops attached to licorice sticks! The streets were crowded. People were everywhere, car horns blaring, tires screeching, half-heard conversations. The sounds of traffic and human frustration packed the air. Nobody looked at each other. People were in too big a hurry just going from here to there. Nothing unusual for the financial district at the end of the day in New York City. This was nothing unusual for New York City – period.

David opened the passenger door and motioned for Bob to get in while Kevin got in on the other side. Once in the car, Bob was trapped in the middle. They rode uptown to Riverside Drive. With rush hour traffic, it took close to an hour to get to their destination. Bob was clenching his jaw and tapping his fingers on both knees. He could feel Kevin glaring at him. David looked out the window.

The only thing on David's mind was his sister, and her kids. He kept thinking about the ugliness of his nephew and niece seeing their father half naked, with some woman other than their mother. If only Victoria hadn't forgotten her book that she and Christopher came back to retrieve, they wouldn't have seen what they saw. Victoria standing at the bedroom door in shock, somehow flipping the bed over according to Catherine! Christopher knocking his father on his ass and the subsequent fist fight they did have a day or so later that Sidney told him about. All of this weighed on David heavily. He knew his sister was drinking also. Stephan had seen her knocking back a few drinks before noon on more than one occasion. She told Stephan the drinks helped her headaches!

The three men rode in tight silence. Although the temperature was in the thirties, Bob had started to sweat. He was so boxed in between Kevin and David he couldn't reach inside his coat pocket for a handkerchief to wipe his forehead. Finally, after one of the longest hours any of them had experienced, they arrived at the condo where Bob and his family lived. The three of them got out of the car before the doorman could get there.

Bob nodded at Casey. "Hey man. How you doing?" He didn't wait for an answer. He kept walking pushed along by a cold wind flying up from the Hudson River. Bob was so absorbed in thought he didn't see Kevin slip the doorman a hundred-dollar bill.

Kevin looked at Casey and said softly, "Thank you. We appreciate your help earlier."

With a bright smile, Casey nodded his head vigorously and said, "Anything for Mrs. Pittman. She's a good woman."

Kevin followed David and Bob into the lobby and onto the elevator. Not a word was said as they rode up to the sixth floor. The elevator door opened and Bob walked straight ahead to the unit he had been living in for almost fifteen years with his wife and children until they left him.

As the men approached the front door, Kevin asked, "You like living in this area? You've got some really nice views of the Hudson River."

"Yeah, I've always liked this part of town," Bob muttered while taking out his keys to open the door. David and Kevin watched him. Bob put his key in the lock. He couldn't turn it. He kept fiddling with it and nothing. He swore under his breath not understanding what the problem was. Perspiration continued to ease across his forehead and now between his nose and upper lip also. He couldn't open his own front door. "What the hell is this?" he said to himself.

David cleared his throat and reached in his pocket for a key. "Bob…"

Bob turned and looked at him clearly irritated. "What?"

"Your key won't work," David said.

"What do you mean my key won't work? This is my condo. What the hell are you talking about?"

"We had the locks changed this morning," David said.

"You had what?"

Kevin put his hand on Bob's shoulder and simply said, "Shhhh… The neighbors have complained to the Condo Association about you. Apparently, you've been having some loud discussions with Cath lately. Keep your voice down."

Bob's eyes widened. He felt violated. By now, David had opened the front door using the new key for the new lock. He stood aside and motioned for everyone to go in. Bob walked in, shoulders almost up to his ears and his mouth getting drier and drier. His footsteps were very deliberate as he plodded down the hall. David and Kevin were right behind him. David was so close to him, Bob could feel David's smooth, even breath. There was a lamp already on in the hallway and another in the living room.

Kevin looked around and smiled. To no one in particular, he said, "Cath was never the best housekeeper, brilliant professor, but no housekeeper."

David grinned for a minute while Bob turned on some more lights and unbuttoned his coat. The lights revealed stacks of magazines and old newspapers piled on the coffee table next to a vase of dying red roses. Right in the middle of the living room was a soccer ball, tennis racket, and some Lacrosse equipment that wasn't there when Bob left for work. Had Catherine and the kids been there, Bob wondered? Books and academic journals were everywhere. There was a contemporary piece of African sculpture in one corner along with several large house plants. In another corner there was something that looked like an African warrior's shield. The wall above the couch held one of Sid's painting. Sidney Anne Barrett, an artist, was Catherine's best friend. The room vibrated with intensity.

Bob took his coat off and threw it on the couch. "Look, what's this about? Catherine and I have had some trouble but it does not warrant you doing all this." He unbuttoned his suit jacket, took off his tie and started to think about making himself a strong drink.

Kevin ordered Bob. "Sit down." Bob didn't move. He just stood there glaring at David and Kevin. Kevin walked over to Bob and repeated himself while putting his hands on Bob's shoulders "encouraging" him to sit. As Bob almost fell into a large, soft leather chair, Kevin continued. "Now, this is how this works tonight. We're going to have a conversation among us, you know, just us men. Then you're going to pack your clothes and leave. All of this disruption is interfering with Victoria and Christopher's schoolwork, you understand? Catherine's afraid they're both going to need some therapy after they witnessed that little escapade you had here."

Bob watched both of them and clenched his fists while a vein on the left side of his forehead started to pulsate. He leaned back in the chair not knowing what else to do.

David walked over to the window and looked out onto Riverside Drive before saying anything. "Bob, we're getting our sister one of the best divorce lawyers in the city. You're not going to have much left when she's done with you."

"And this divorce is based on what?!" Bob looked at the liquor cabinet for a quick minute. He exhaled and shook his head from left to right a few times. "What has Catherine told you?" Bob demanded. He held his head in his hand for a moment taken aback by a throbbing headache.

Kevin glared at Bob eyes wide with disbelief.

"We can start with adultery," said Kevin who was now standing in front of Bob. "Then you went crazy and started slapping Cath around. That was like puttin' a noose around your neck," Kevin said. Looking down directly at Bob, Kevin said, "Look at me. Look at me! Open your eyes, damn it!"

Bob lifted his head, opened his eyes, and looked at Kevin. "What?"

David walked up behind the chair where Bob was sitting and put his hands on Bob's shoulders. Bob jumped.

Kevin calmly said, "Pay attention. I only want to say this once. You ever lay a hand on our sister again, you will die. Don't even look at the kids cross-eyed."

Squeezing Bob's shoulders, David said, "Accidents happen, Bob. You've worked too hard man. It would be a shame if you had an accident, ya' know?" David walked in front of Bob and stood next to Kevin. "But I'm a fair man. Why don't you tell us what you think has happened? There're two sides to every story." David then sat on the couch while Bob sat up in his chair that was across from David. No one sensed there was the invisible presence of another life in the room, a tall, well-dressed man of indeterminate age, calmly watching from the corner behind Bob.

"This is none of your business," Bob said to both of them. He suddenly looked behind him. He saw nothing and turned back around.

"Oh, but it is," said David. "The minute you hit our sister, it became our business, and when she walked in on you and that 'girl' in her bed in her house? And then the kids saw it too? This is not just about you and Catherine. It is now the business of the entire Stockard family." David looked at his watch. "You got about two hours, maybe a little less to state your case and get packed."

"And then what? The sky falls?" Bob didn't know what David was going to do next. He didn't know what either one of them were going to do and he couldn't shake the feeling that someone or something else was there too.

Before Bob could speak, Kevin said, "We've made arrangements to have your stuff taken out of here tonight. Catherine doesn't want to be reminded of you, and please take the bed."

"What?" Bob's breathing was shallow and rapid. He looked over his shoulder again to the corner.

"What the hell's the matter with you?" David asked. "You having a panic attack?"

"No! What do you mean, you've made arrangements?

Hell, with you... Look, you know our property has to be divided..."

"No, don't even go there. Don't start becoming a lawyer now. You forget who you're talking to! You put another woman in my sister's marriage bed. The Stockards are old fashioned. You're faithful. If you can't be faithful, get a divorce. It's simple but don't put another woman in her bed!" David's eyes examined Bob.

Bob was looking in every corner of the room. He started biting his lower lip.

"Why are you so nervous? Are you hiding your little friend in here somewhere?" David asked, his mouth slightly opened in disbelief at the thought.

"There's nobody here. I swear," Bob said.

David looked right through him. "Man, if you're lying... we'll find out shortly because the movers are on their way."

"The movers?!" Bob shifted in his seat. "You're inviting a world of trouble, Mr. Fancy Lawyer."

"Don't worry about me. You know I can talk my way out of this. I didn't go to Harvard Law for nothing." David paused. "Okay, let's go. We've got a storage facility picked out. Your stuff can stay there as long as you want," Kevin said.

"And where am I supposed to stay?" Bob asked.

David pulled out an envelope from his inside coat pocket. He opened it and spread its contents on the coffee table, a half dozen plus, color photos of Bob and a young woman kissing on the sidewalk, walking into an apartment building, having lunch in a restaurant, grocery shopping, etc. Looking at the photos for a minute, David looked at Bob and said while pointing out the young woman in the photos, "You can stay with her."

Bob saw the photos and his eyes grew wide with disgust at himself. He got up, walked over to the liquor cabinet, took out a bottle of Scotch, and a glass. Carefully, he poured himself some and then added a small amount of club soda in the glass. He took a slow sip and let the liquid slide past his dry tongue and down his throat while he eyed the room once more. The fact that he hated Scotch never stopped him from drinking it. Glass in hand, Bob turned and looked first at David, who was still seated, and then Kevin, who was now looking out the window at the river.

Kevin turned, his eyes motionless, and asked Bob, "Okay, can we get going? No b.s., just straight talk. David and I need to hear something from you, and we need to hear it now."

"And what good will that do me? You seem to have it all figured out." Bob drank the rest of his Scotch and soda and sat down in his chair.

David gazed at his brother-in-law. David's face was calm, like still waters, the opposite of Bob's face. David's eyes slowly studied his brother-in-law before he said anything. Kevin was now standing behind Bob's chair. Taking a deep breath, David said, "You know, I'm a defense lawyer, right?"

Bob glared at him and said, "Who doesn't?"

Kevin put his hand on Bob's shoulder and said, "Kill the attitude."

"Most people have heard about the scandalous cases I've handled involving white collar crime. But I've also defended some very sketchy characters. You can forget the Mafia. This is a whole new breed of criminal, high tech, international, munitions, corporate espionage, biological weapons, 21st century stuff. It's deep. I figure if I can make the legal system work for them, I improve the chances of the system working for the average brother, you know? Anyway, that's a longer conversation. These new criminals have two things in common with the old criminals. They know how to kill people, and they know how to repay a favor beyond writing a check. If I wanted you dead, all I have to do is pick up the phone and call, you understand? Now, you need to tell us something that makes sense before we leave here tonight, otherwise I may have to make a phone call."

"You're threatening me? What do you think this is, The Godfather?" Bob asked. He realized that his body was rigid from tension.

David threw his arms open, smiled and said with great bravado, "No, no, no! I'm not threatening you. Not at all." He then leaned forward and patted Bob's knee before continuing. "Listen, I'm just explaining one of the options I have if you don't start making some real sense," David said.

"What happened?" Kevin asked. "When did things start to go south between you and our sister?"

Bob closed his eyes, took a deep breath, and let it out slowly. He really didn't want to talk to them or anybody else. His marriage was his business and Bob resented the Stockards. "The marriage didn't go south, Catherine went south."

Kevin asked, "Are you saying this is Catherine's fault? That somehow she hit herself and then arranged for you to have an affair or a fling or whatever it was or is with that young woman in the photo?"

"Say something," David said.

Bob sat there, a headache beginning to sharply bang his brains, and a low-grade sense of terror was paralyzing him. He bit his lower lip, looked at them for a long minute, and then blurted out, "She's too damn black, too big. She's an embarrassment to me, especially now."

David jumped up and yelled, "Whoa!!!" He put his hands behind his head and locked his fingers. "Have you looked at yourself? Kevin is a brown skinned man. You and I are dark skinned, man. None of us would ever be mistaken for anything other than black and Catherine's too black for you?"

"You asked. And she's too damned close to Sid. I swear to God, there's three of us in this marriage. She cares more about her than she does me. I'm sick of it. Sick of feeling like I'm way down on her list. I've got stature now and she isn't helping. She doesn't even recognize me for what I've become." Bob was unable to look at Kevin or David.

They stared at each other. Eventually David said to his brother-in-law, "That's some crazy-assed shit. Man, what are you saying? Now that you've made it, the woman who helped put you through law school, gave birth to your two children, is suddenly too black for you? Is that what you're saying? Am I really hearing this? This is about as original as one of those Japanese monster movies with the large lizards."

"Look, I asked her to stop wearing the braids. She wouldn't do it. I asked her to stop talking about politics all the time around the other partners and associates at the office parties. She wouldn't do it."

Kevin broke in and said, "She's a political science professor! What do you expect her to talk about? Baking bread, fashion? C'mon!"

"I want the same kind of wife the rest of 'em have," Bob said.

"And what kind is that?" David asked.

"White! Polished, quiet, slim…" He paused for a minute. "She's the reason it took me so long to make partner in the first place."

David's eyes became laser beams directed at his brother-in-law. "Did anybody ever tell you you're a sick son of a bitch? You drank all the Kool Aid! You couldn't even go out and find one of those light-skinned sisters with the 'good hair' and the designer clothes who belonged to Jack & Jill when they were growing up. I'll be damned."

Bob wanted to beat both of them, turn them into piles of mashed muscles, but all he could do is glare back at David.

"What you really want is some woman who's deferential. Cath defers to nobody! She's been outspoken all her life. She came flying out of the womb with opinions! I know. I'm her big brother! You think she's going to change because you're a partner in some law firm? You are insane. And by the way, Cath is going to stay black, just like the three of us in this room. She won't be able or willing to change her color to suit your career plans! So, you got a problem, my brother. A big one!"

Bob jumped up and said, "Listen, I need somebody who's going to support me, make me look good, be what I want her to be." He looked around for the bottle of Scotch.

All three of them just stood in silence for several seconds.

Kevin looked at Bob and said, "Something about this isn't adding up. You and Catherine been married a long time. She was outspoken when you married her. She had braids when you married her. She was black when you married her. So, what really changed. What are you not telling us?"

Bob didn't say anything. He made himself another drink and sat down. David perched himself on the end of the coffee table right in front of the chair where Bob was seated. David leaned forward so he could look Bob right in the eye. "You really need to say something, and it better make sense. This foolishness with the braids, and the outspoken quality Catherine has…and this hostile, fixation you've got on Sidney… It's all been around from day one. Do you really think we believe this is the whole story? Remember what I do for a living."

David reached back and picked up the photos he had shown earlier and held them in his hand while looking at Bob. Holding the photos up so Bob could see them, David said, "This happened."

Bob's head felt close to exploding. "Yeah," he mumbled. "I met someone…her."

Kevin motioned to his brother to give him some of the photos. He looked at them again and said to Bob, "Are you talking about this?" he asked while pointing to the young woman in the photo. "She's 'twelve'! She's got to be half your age. Have you given your daughter any thought while you were doing this?"

"…and this young lady is very white," David said. "That fantasy is fulfilled. What does she do?"

"She buys art for corporations."

"Hmph," David said. "And you met this little girl where?"

"At one of Sid's shows. It was a group show somewhere," Bob said.

David looked at his brother and said, "Well, I'll be damned. How long has this been going on?"

"Almost three years, maybe," Bob said and then sipped some scotch. "She's very smart, fun to be around…"

"This was the woman who was here when the kids walked in?" Kevin asked?

Bob froze, terrified.

"Hey! I'm asking you a question," Kevin repeated.

Bob whispered, "No. That was someone else. She lives in the building."

A few seconds passed. Kevin looked up at the ceiling and shook his head. David took a deep breath, slowly exhaled, and said, "You need to start packing your things. Give one of them a call. Decide and tell her you'll be over later." Saying more to himself than anyone else, David muttered, "I keep waiting for a black man to do something original like leave a white woman for a black woman. This is the oldest story in the book, the very oldest…" He stared into space hurting for his sister, before saying anything more. "Two…damn. Bob, start packing."

Kevin walked over to Bob and said, "Before you start packing, how did you end up hitting our sister?"

Bob felt his stomach twist. "I got angry one night…that's all it was."

"What do you mean, that's all it was?" Kevin asked. "You don't hit women because you're mad at them! You lay a hand on my sister again…" A loud noise came from the back of the condo.

The three men suddenly stopped talking and became motionless.

"What was that?" Kevin asked.

"Sounded like furniture being dragged across the floor," David said. He looked at Bob and said, "One of them is here isn't she?"

"No," Bob whispered. "Man, I'm telling you."

"Maybe she's trying to sneak out through the service entrance, tripped over something. That would be something," David said and smirked.

At that moment, every light in the condo went out. The radio in the living room suddenly turned on. Jazz tumbled out through the speakers, sputtering with intermittent static.

"Stay here. I'm going to take a look," Kevin said to Bob and David. It took him a few seconds for his eyes to adjust to the darkness.

"No. Kev, we'll all go," David said. "Something's not right."

"I'm not going anywhere," Bob said.

"Call the police, Bob," David said. There was another loud noise as if a pile of books dropped. Kevin flew down the hall to the bedrooms with Olympic speed.

"Phone's not working," Bob mumbled.

"What?" David asked dumbfounded. "What happened?"

"Static," Bob mumbled. "Cell phone is just…dead."

David and Bob heard Kevin cry out. David ran down the hall. Bob sat in the living room unable to move. Then he looked up and saw it. Now, Bob was unable to scream.

David followed the noise to Victoria's bedroom. The door was half open. David saw Kevin looking in Victoria's room. He was riveted on what he saw. David heard movement from inside Victoria's room. It sounded as if more than one person was in there. Kevin cautiously finished opening Vic's bedroom door terrified by what he had already seen. David didn't know what he would discover.

The lights started to flicker again making it difficult to really witness what was going on. Within seconds the lights stopped flickering and went on. Then David and Kevin saw them.

"Jesus Christ," David said under his breath.

"What the hell..." Kevin was barely breathing. Standing on the far side of Victoria's room, behind her desk, were three gray beings, non-human, small in stature, almost frail looking except for their large heads and very large, black, almond shaped eyes. Somehow David thought their eyes had the power to communicate in a way unknown to him and maybe anybody else who was human. They felt friendly. They felt almost kind but neither Kevin nor David understood how they knew this, much less if they could trust what they were seeing and feeling.

"We're not here to hurt you. We're here to get some of Victoria's things." That was said but not out loud. Kevin and David "heard" it in their minds.

David swallowed and started to ask, "Why are…"

He was cut off by another one of them. "Victoria is our student and our relative. She's family."

Kevin leaned back against the wall, covered his face with his hand, closed his eyes, and thought, "This is my imagination. This isn't real."

The third being walked over to Kevin. It barely came up to Kevin's waist. "Open your eyes, Kevin."

Kevin's hand dropped, and his eyes flipped open. The being extended its thin, long finger and gently poked Kevin. His mouth fell open.

"We're real," the being said and softly smiled. "Tell them we gave you the 'poke test' so everyone knows we're real." It turned to David and conveyed to him, "We've been watching over Victoria. We would let nothing happen to her. She's had some close calls but we were always nearby if things became dire. She's very precious to us. We will now take care of everything. There are others coming for her."

The fourth being walked in from the living room. There was a cute clumsiness to their walk that made David want to smile. This one wasn't gray, but pale beige and a little taller than the others. It looked up at David and smiled, as best as possible, with its tiny mouth that looked like a slit. It walked over to the three other beings. David and Kevin looked at each other. They knew the beings were "talking" to each other telepathically. It was something Kevin didn't want to believe, but that's what was happening. The Beings turned and looked at the Stockard brothers for a moment, nodded to Kevin and David, and then walked through the wall with several of Victoria's books and notebooks, leaving Kevin and David in some form of shock, without any reference points, without much understanding. Their reality was shattered.

Back in the living room, Bob had peed on himself.

CHAPTER NINE
The Aftermath

Kevin and David walked back to the living room and sat in silence. It was hard to tell if they were still breathing. The lights were back on. The radio was absent of static. Bob was teary eyed as he looked around. His body shook unevenly, reminding you of after-shocks of a major earthquake.

"Man, what the fuck just happened?" Bob finally asked. His voice was barely above a whisper. "What was that thing I saw, and you're telling me there were more in Victoria's bedroom? I'd rather deal with the Klan than whatever those things were." Bob's shaking increased.

Kevin looked at him and noticed Bob's pants. "Bob, go clean yourself up, man."

"The cushion... I mean..." Bob couldn't finish the sentence. He was staring into space.

"Don't worry about it. We'll take care of it. Go. Clean yourself up," David said.

"I can't stop shaking." Kevin helped Bob stand. Barely able to walk, he took a few steps and asked. "You're sure they're gone?"

"They walk through walls. You can't be sure of anything," David said. "Please go. Put on some clean pants. The movers are still coming." David was unusually calm. He had seen these beings somewhere else but he couldn't remember when nor where. They were familiar and that jolted him! That jolt propelled him to the back of the couch. He stared into empty space. As quickly as he leaned back, he managed to lean forward, put his head in his hand and began mouthing the Lord's Prayer.

Bob reluctantly walked into his bedroom. Kevin returned to Victoria's room looking for something, anything that would explain what just happened. He sat on her bed, clutched the down comforter and carefully looked around. Convinced "they" were gone, Kevin wept. He heard himself whisper, "Mama, Mama, Mama, what the hell happened here?" He curled up into the fetal position and continued to whisper. "Victoria, baby girl, who are you? What are you? What if they come back?" Kevin stayed in his niece's room for almost ten minutes. It took him that long to compose himself.

The three men gathered in the living room. They sat in silence for what felt like hours, each one lost in thought.

"I need another drink," Bob murmured. He stood, weakly walked to the liquor cabinet. "I told you Victoria was a freak. Been trying to tell Catherine that. Victoria is not my child."

Bob's words broke the spell of shock and disbelief they were experiencing. Kevin grabbed Bob and threw him on the couch like a rag doll. Standing over him, Kevin said, "I don't pretend to know what just happened, okay? Something happened. But I know this much, my niece is no freak. My sister gave you everything she had and then some, and if I hear you say another word about Victoria or Christopher, I'll beat the shit out of you. Don't even think about looking cross-eyed at Christopher. Are we clear?"

"Yeah, we're clear," Bob said. He started shaking again.

"We've got to pull ourselves together," David said. "The movers are coming."

"What are we going to do?" Bob asked. "We're just supposed to snap back? I can't do this."

"You better find a way, my brother," Kevin said. "We better all find a way. We gotta cope."

"Maybe it was a dream," Bob said quietly. "Maybe we were hallucinating."

David looked at Bob and rhetorically asked, "All three of us? The same dream? The same hallucination? Where does that happen?"

Bob started to gasp for air while thinking. Slowly, he got up to fix himself another drink. He looked to Kevin and David for guidance, for anything to help him make sense out of what he saw and felt. His fear was cloaked in questions they were all asking themselves. The dampness in the seat of his pants was a reminder of the reality all three of them experienced.

"What do I do with all this? Huh?! 'Da hell happened here? Who are they? Where did they come from? Are they coming back? How do they exist? They told me somebody else was coming. 'Da hell is this? And who the fuck is going to believe us? We can't tell anybody about this. Not a soul! They'll think we're stark raving nuts and have another reason to put us away. What do we do?" Bob asked.

David inhaled, then slowly exhaled, looked at Bob and said, "We keep going. We cope, 'cause that's what Black people do."

Kevin looked directly at Bob and yanked him up from his seat so suddenly you wondered if it happened at all. The glass of scotch fell to the floor as Kevin backed Bob up against the nearest wall and put his forearm against Bob's throat. David watched with uncharacteristic indifference.

"I'm not so traumatized by whatever just happened that I forgot why we're here in the first place," Kevin said. "The only reason I'm going to let you live and not break your neck tonight is because I don't want to go to jail. I'm not going to put my friends and family through that agony. But understand this, and I know we've said it at least twice, but I'm going to say it again. If we ever find out you've laid a hand on Catherine or those kids after tonight…" Bob tried to nod his head to indicate he understood, but he couldn't. Kevin suddenly removed his arm from Bob's neck. He lurched forward coughing trying to get his breath back. Somehow, he found enough energy to go to the bedroom and find some clean his pants.

The intercom buzzer rang. Hearing it, Bob collapsed where he stood. His heart thumped like a bass drum. Kevin started pounding his fist into the open palm of this other hand. He suppressed his need to scream and do great harm to anyone! David stood, bent over for a second or two, and then stood as upright as possible. He cleared his throat, checked his posture one more time, let out a deep sigh, and in a flash, regained his "cool, calm, in charge demeanor." He walked down the hall cautiously and answered the intercom. Within minutes, the movers were at the front door. Kevin and Bob heard David say, "The movers are here." David escorted them into the living room."

It was going to be a long night.

CHAPTER TEN
Leaving

Wearing clean underwear and a fresh pair of pants, Bob dragged himself into the kitchen while the movers were talking to David. Bob couldn't face anybody! Looking out the kitchen window into the darkness of a workday night, he threw two aspirin in his mouth followed by a small glass of water. He jerked his head back to swallow the pills. His hands were still trembling. His mind couldn't register what he was looking at, a sidewalk, a highway, a river, lights… What did it matter given what he had just been through and what he had seen? He felt his heart continue to thump, a bit short of bursting through his shirt and sweater. Bob took another deep breath and let it out very slowly. He remembered that he had forgotten to take his blood pressure pills…again.

"The movers are here," Kevin said.

Bob, knees turning to Jell-O, wanted to collapse. His shoulders sagged. His strength trickled out through his feet. He felt like a dishrag rung dry. There was nothing left. Slowly he turned around, leaned against the kitchen sink and saw Kevin.

"Did you think we were making this up? You need to tell these people what to take," Kevin said. He saw the bottle of aspirin on the kitchen counter. He picked it up, glanced at it and then looked at Bob. "It's going to take more than aspirin to take care of you."

Bob stared at Kevin for a moment. He said nothing and walked past Kevin back to the living room. There were three huge men standing in the living room talking to David. As

Bob approached, the conversation stopped. All eyes were on Bob. He couldn't see the look on his face. It was a cross between terror and madness.

David said, "Bob, meet Mickey Harrison," pointing to a burly guy with shocking red hair and freckles. "And this gentleman," David said pointing to a smaller man who looked like he had worked out every day of his life, either at a gym or in prison. "This is Alfred Watson and next to him is Ben Fairchild." Ben looked like he could literally move mountains. His eyes were sizing up the room.

Bob nodded at them.

Alfred, adjusting his bandana, made a rumbling noise of recognition, barely decipherable, and Ben raised his hand in acknowledgment.

Mickey looked at Bob and said, "We're ready when you are. Tell us what's going, what has to be packed." Ben had left a stack of moving boxes along with several wardrobe boxes in the hallway.

Bob looked at David and asked, "What do I do with my books? My photographs?"

"I don't know. That's up to you. But remember, it's unlikely you will come back here for anything," David said.

Bob looked at the movers and said, "Okay. Let me show you what has to be done." Bob's clothes were rapidly packed in wardrobe boxes. It would take several days to pack his books and the photographs he had been collecting for over a decade. It was obvious Bob would have to work something out with Catherine or her lawyer to get the remainder of his things. That thought made him crazy all over again. He was going to need his own lawyer. It was clear. And then he remembered he had to go to Victoria's school to meet with

Ms. Butterfield and some guy named Charles Solomon in a few days. He cursed underneath his breath.

David and Kevin watched the movers and Bob. Kevin asked him, "Do you want anything else, anything from the living room?"

"No, this is it." Bob said, trying not to hyperventilate.

"Okay," said David as he stood. "Let's bring your luggage and garment bags down to the car."

"The car is still here?" Bob asked.

"We've got it for as long as we want. So, we'll put your suitcase and everything in the trunk, and then we'll take you wherever you'll be staying. Should we go to the little girl's house? The art consultant? We know where she lives."

Bob felt his head on the verge of splitting right down the middle. He stared at David and Kevin with all the contempt he could muster. David looked at his brother-in-law as Bob placed his right hand on his forehead as if to hold his brains in his skull.

"Bob, don't come back here," David ordered.

"After tonight, you think I want to come back here?!"

"So long as you know your life with our sister is over. Her lawyer will call you. Work out the details. Maybe you can mediate a settlement, but that's it, Jack," Kevin said. "Gotta get going.

You've got a meeting with Brendan tomorrow morning, remember?"

"You think I can meet with somebody after what happened tonight?" Bob said as he put on his coat. "What about what happened here tonight with those…"

David, serene as a stone that had seen millions of years go by asked, "What about it? Until we find out what happened, we haven't seen a damned thing. Kevin, did you see anything?"

"Not a thing," Kevin said.

Bob was lost. "Are they coming back?"

"I don't know," David said.

"What am I supposed to do?" Bob was on the verge of tears.

"Get your ass outta here," Kevin said. His voice was glacial. "Let's keep our priorities straight."

CHAPTER ELEVEN
It's Getting Complicated

David was finally alone in the back seat of the car. Bob insisted on being dropped off at a hotel, and Kevin had been driven to his condo on Central Park West. David had one more stop to make before he could go home. Home was an understated but beautiful six-bedroom house in Riverdale. He reached in his pocket for his cell phone to call his wife, Lisbeth. She would be worried. David knew that Lisbeth wasn't so sure about this "intervention." It made her nervous. She had never liked Bob Pittman. David thought, "If this intervention made Lisbeth nervous. How in the hell am I going to tell her about what else happened this evening?"

Lisbeth had put two of their four kids to bed, Geoff and Arianna. The other two, fraternal twin brothers, Maxwell and Larry, were still doing homework. Lisbeth answered the phone and said, "Hello?"

"Hey Babe…" David said quietly.

"Hey, are you okay? What happened?" Lisbeth asked.

"We got him out. He decided to stay at a hotel and that's fine with me. I don't care where he stays so long as it's not in the condo. I gotta call the attorney I found for Cath tomorrow."

"Are you on your way home now?"

"No, I've got to stop and see her. Let her know what's happened," David said.

"You sound so… tired. You sound funny. Can't you come home and call her?"

"I could, but I don't want to. I'd rather see her. It won't

take very long. I should be home before midnight. How are you?"

"Oh, I'm fine. Two surgeries." Lisbeth said. "Everything's quiet, really."

Listening to David, she couldn't shake that undercurrent she heard in his voice. His tone was off. Lisbeth filed it away until he came home and filled her in on more of what happened earlier.

She remembered the first time she went to Riverdale, specifically the Fieldston area to see the house they ended up buying. This part of Riverdale was like some photo spread in an upscale magazine. There were cobble stone roads, Embassy residences, beautiful homes and lots of trees. There were prestigious private schools scattered at various entrances to Fieldston like sentinels on watch. The Riverdale Country Day School was at one end, at the other, The Horace Mann School. She never imagined living in a section of New York City like this. It was hard to believe you were still in the city much less the Bronx. Riverdale is in the Bronx the same way Bel Air is in Los Angeles.

She smiled remembering how David would boast that when traffic was moving, you could drive from Riverdale to mid-town Manhattan in roughly twenty to twenty-five minutes. The Henry Hudson Parkway led directly to the West Side Highway and it was a straight shot into the heart of Manhattan. Lisbeth thought how well this community of very successful, high-income, low key professionals, suited her husband. There were only two other African American families on Fieldston Road. It was a rarified neighborhood, and she still felt uncomfortable there.

They chatted until David was in front of Sidney's

brownstone. As the car pulled up, David put his cell phone away and reached for the cross he always wore around his neck, regardless. David started softly saying a prayer of thanks. He was grateful that his family was in-tact. He was grateful his brother, Kevin, didn't break Bob's neck earlier. Kevin's appearance was somewhat deceiving; because he was lean people underestimated Kevin's strength until it was too late. David knew that Kevin could've snapped Bob's neck in two like a twig. But those strange, grey beings. It was hard to "unsee" them now. David took a deep breath and barely whispered, "God, what just happened? Give me the strength to get through this…please. Tell me how to hold the impossible. What were those things we encountered?" Images of these little grey creatures scampered across his mind again and again.

The driver said to David, "Mr. Stockard, we're here." The driver heard no response and turned to look at Bob. "Mr. Stockard?"

David jumped slightly. "Okay, Thank you. My mind wandered off. If you want to go have a cup of coffee or something while I'm here, that's okay. I can text you when I'm ready to go."

"Thank you," the driver said.

"Not a problem," David said as he got out of the car. He shut the car door firmly, paused and then walked up to Sidney's front door. He knew all about Sidney and Stephan. All of New York City knew about them. "Stephan knew how to take care of somebody he loved," David thought. "As opposed to this fool my sister married." David rang the bell and heard Sidney's cocker spaniels barking.

Sidney opened the door, holding both of her spaniels by the collar. "David! It's been awhile. Come in," Sidney said as she closed the door and let go of her spaniels who started to sniff David's shoes.

He hugged Sid and said, "Girl, let me look at you?" He held her at arm's length, smiling. "How're you doing? For real? I know it's been rough."

"David, I'm fine, really. C'mon, Catherine's downstairs. The kids have gone to bed." Sidney stopped for a second and searched his face, "You okay?"

"Yeah. It's just been a long day and dealing with Bob. I'll tell you about it later."

Sidney said. "Bob can wear on your nerves after the first three minutes."

David snickered, followed Sidney and said, "Shoot, life can suck sometimes. Listen, if you need anything…" David said.

"Thank you, but I'm okay. Give me your coat." The spaniels were still watching David.

"No, I'm not going to stay long. I just wanted to talk to Cath," he said.

"We're downstairs in the kitchen."

Sid led him to the garden level where the kitchen and dining room were. He looked around and smiled thinking, "This is Sidney, style and class."

"When did you move in here?" David asked as they walked downstairs.

"We moved in about six months before we got married. It was right after Labor Day," Sid responded.

"Wow…place looks good."

"Stephan so loved coming home at the end of a day…

I..." Sid paused and didn't finish the sentence.

David gently grabbed her hand and said quietly, "I know it's hard."

As they walked into the kitchen, Catherine walked over and hugged David. "Hey, big brother."

David grinned at his sister and touched the side of her face. "You okay? For real now."

"I'm getting' there. Come on. Sit down." She pointed to a stool at the kitchen island. "You look funny. I don't mean, ha-ha funny. I mean funny as in a little off. Was it that stressful dealing with Bob?"

"Bob can be a real jerk. We had some unexpected… difficulties, anomalies. Sid, you got any herbal tea?" David asked as he scanned the kitchen. Looking at Sid, he said, "Lisbeth would love this kitchen, not that we didn't spend a small fortune doing over ours… But this is nice. This is you."

"Thank you. Cath there's some peppermint and ginger tea in the cabinet next to the stove. You know where everything is. I'm going to leave you two alone to talk. I'll be upstairs."

"You don't have to leave," Catherine said. "Damn, we ain't got no secrets anymore!" They all laughed.

David muttered to himself, "Not quite…"

"I know," Sid said, "but I'm going anyway." She turned around and saw Victoria coming down the stairs. Sidney was surprised. "Vic, what are you doing up?"

"I came down to see Uncle David," Victoria said. She looked sleepy.

"How did you know he was here, Victoria?" Catherine asked.

Victoria stared blankly at her mother before saying

anything, "I just did. Uncle David and I have to have a private conversation."

"We do?" David asked. "You should be in bed. What if I walk you back to your bedroom?"

Sidney was watching this interaction like a surgeon preparing to cut open a patient.

"No. The living room is fine," Victoria said.

Victoria and David went upstairs and sat on the couch. She turned her small body to look directly at her uncle. "You met some of my friends tonight. Don't be scared. They won't hurt you unless you try to hurt them. Please don't."

"Your friends? What are you talking about sweetheart?"

"Uncle David, don't test me," Victoria said and frowned.

He shook his head for a minute. "Sweetheart, how do you know these things?"

"I just do. Don't tell Mom, she'll freak out, but you can tell Aunt Sidney. Things are going to be changing right before Christmas."

"Vic, who exactly are these friends of yours? Where're they from?"

"Most of them are from another planet. But some of them are from another realm, another dimension."

David took a deep breath and let the air out slowly before asking Victoria another question. "How did you meet them?"

"They came to visit when I was a little girl," Victoria said.

David smiled and put his arm around her. They leaned back letting the soft pillows comfort them. David's head was beginning to pound.

"Sweetheart, you're still a little girl. How little?" he asked.

"Very little," Victoria said firmly.

"Why? Why did they come to see you," David asked and kissed her on the head.

"Because we're family, Uncle David." Both of them sat in silence. David closed his eyes as if that would prevent any additional incredible information from bashing its way into his brain. He had to change the conversation. Aliens visiting his niece was more than he wanted to handle. David was barely holding on.

"Vic, I saw your father tonight. He's left the condo. But I'm sure he'll work something out with your mother so you and Chris can see him."

Victoria turned into her uncle's arms and said, "I don't ever want to see him again, Uncle David." She unexpectedly sprang to her feet. "I'm going to bed. Don't forget what I said." And she left, leaving her uncle to ponder everything that had happened. He took another deep breath and let it out slowly.

When he returned to the kitchen, Catherine asked, "What's going on? Is Vic okay? What did she tell you?"

"You wouldn't believe me if I told you. Later, okay? But right now, I want to talk to you."

"My cue to leave," said Sidney. "Call me when you finish." Sidney, Bonwit and Coco, floated up the stairs.

David turned and watched her. Looking back at his sister he said, tongue in cheek, "That's her uniform, isn't it? Faded jeans, a turtleneck covered by an oversized white shirt. "Can she get any smaller? What is she? A size two?!"

Catherine poked her brother and they both watched as Sid continued to float up the stairs with the large shirt ballooning out behind her like a royal robe.

Sid turned around and yelled, "I heard that!" They all laughed.

While fixing tea for her brother, Catherine asked, "So, what's the story? Is he gone?"

"I told you this morning we were going to get him out of there, and we did. You can go home, sis. He's gone. We changed the locks on the front door and the service entrance. The Condo Association knows he's no longer welcomed on the premises. All the doormen have his photo, and we're going to get that restraining order first thing tomorrow morning anyway. But if the fool shows up, the doormen know to call the police. He's taken his clothes, his desk and the bedroom furniture." David reached in his coat pocket and gave his sister the new set of keys and a business card. "I'm contacting this divorce lawyer for you first thing in the morning. She's the best, Cath. That's her card. You need to call tomorrow afternoon, understand? She'll be expecting to hear from you. Don't let this hang." David started to sip his tea.

Catherine looked at her brother's hands. They were shaking. "David, what's going on?"

"What do you mean?"

"Your hands are shaking."

David looked at his hands, set the tea down and said, "It's nothing. I'm just tired, Cath."

"Ahuh..." Catherine said still looking at his hands. She paused. Her brother just didn't look right. "I've never seen your hands shake."

"Sis, I'm fine. All I need is some sleep."

"Okay. How did you know things were...so bad?" Cath asked. "I didn't tell Mom. I didn't tell anybody. I mean Sidney knew sort of. Vic and Chris came over here one day when Bob..."

"You didn't have to tell anybody. Mom saw the bruises ... and Sidney called me."

"Sidney called you?! I didn't know the two of you were that kind of close," Catherine said.

"Yeah. There's a lot you don't know, little sister!"

Catherine stood for a minute, staring into space and began to cry. David put his tea down and got up to hug his sister. "It's going to be all right. Don't cry, please."

"What did I do wrong, David? What did I do wrong?"

"Nothing." He saw a box of Kleenex and pulled out a few for Catherine. "Here, wipe those eyes and blow your nose. Come on, before the ugly cry starts," and he smiled at his sister. "You're not alone. You got your family. Sid's here. We're all here for you and the kids. Don't forget that."

Blowing her nose, she looked at David and said, "Thank you. You know I love you to death."

"No thanks needed. This is what we do, right? We take care of each other. We watch over each other. That's what family does anyway. If Dad were still here this is what he would want done. Okay?"

She nodded her head.

"Sis, just let us know whatever you want to do. It's okay with us. But I gotta bad feeling about your husband."

"What do you mean?" Cath asked. "You're beginning to sound like Sid."

"No, no. C'mon now, Sid's in another category entirely. She's Counselor Troi! Star Trek's got nothing on Sid! You know it and I know it."

"Granted, but what do you mean? What's your feeling?" Catherine asked.

"I don't know what I mean. I just got this bad feeling. And listen, you better call, Mom." David kissed his sister goodbye before they walked up the stairs.

"David, you look funny." Catherine bit her lower lip.

"What the hell does that mean?" David asked jokingly.

"You get that funny way about you when you're preoccupied with something."

"I'm fine – for real – just got a lot on my mind. Work. I've got some research to do and I'm not quite sure how I'm going to do it. But, don't worry about me. It's you and the kids we need to take care of." David texted his driver.

Catherine looked intently at her brother before saying, "Okay, if you say so. You would let us know if something was really wrong, wouldn't you?"

"Yes! One more thing, you get some counseling, for real. Ask Sidney to suggest someone. She knows a lot of those people. Somebody for you and the kids. I don't want Chris turning into an axe murderer! Too much of Kevin in Chris!"

Catherine smiled and said, "It's a deal."

"Okay, I'm going to hold you to that. I gotta go."

Once upstairs, he looked for Sid who was in the living room reading. "Sid, I'm going," David said.

Sid met him in the hall. "I'm glad you came by."

"Me too. Listen don't be a stranger. You know you're family. We'd love to see you at the house." He put his arm around her as they walked to the front door and said, "Thank you for all this, for taking care of Catherine and the kids. It means a lot to us. You mean a lot to us."

Sid smiled. "You don't have to thank me. You know that. Look, we'll talk. The holidays are coming. We'll work something out. And David, you get some rest also. You look tired."

Hugging her, David said, "I will and don't lie! I expect to see you, if not for Thanksgiving then Christmas. Just come. Riverdale's a lot closer than the Hudson River Valley! You don't have to call. Bring your four-legged companions too." Looking at his sister he said, "Cath, make this happen." Buttoning his coat, he told them good-bye.

Sid locked the door behind him, looked at Catherine and

said, "Your family is a real gift."

She nodded her head and said, "Sid, I need your help."

CHAPTER TWELVE
Victoria's Notes

I had to tell Uncle David about my friends that he met this evening. Some of them are my siblings! I'm afraid he's going to need some time to process all of this. But I wanted him to know they would never hurt him unless he did something to me. He said he understood. I'm not so sure. I think they scared him. Why do people get all crazy just because someone looks different from them?

But the really big news is Aunt Sidney's making Mom go to a shrink! I overheard Aunt Sidney talking to her! OMG! Mom is going to hate that, but she'll go anyway. She usually does whatever Aunt Sidney says.

I should be asleep. But I'm worried about Mom and Dad meeting with Ms. Butterfield. Mr. Solomon's supposed to be there. He's an amazing man. I don't know why he can't be my father. There's something very wonderful about him. He's smart and strong and I've never met anyone like him. I just have a feeling about him. It would be great if my feeling was right. This might be a good time to pray. I understand prayer. It's not like Gram's prayer. This is different but prayer works. So, I'm going to pray. I've decided to create a new family. Wait until I tell Chris that he has additional sibs also. It's the parents that have to go, especially Dad.

Gotta go. Somebody's coming down the hallway! They think I'm asleep!

CHAPTER THIRTEEN
David Gets Home

David quietly closed the front door and walked into the living room. He dropped his coat and briefcase on the couch, stepped out of his shoes, slowly sat down, and held his head in his hands. It was after midnight. The house was silent. The living room was shadowy from the light of one lamp. His wife, Lisbeth, had turned this impressive house into a safe haven for him and their children. Until tonight he felt relatively out of harm's way, and secure in his home, as much as any black family in America can be. But after tonight, after what he'd seen, and he knew what he saw, nothing would ever be the same. Everything he knew about the world and what was possible and impossible was shattered. The very definition of reality was crushed from his perspective.

"David?"

He looked up and found Lisbeth standing there.

"Babe, you okay?" Lisbeth asked.

"Hey sweetheart," David said. "Cute pajamas." He extended his hand and she sat next to him. He kissed her and smiled. "I am so lucky to have you."

"I know that," she said playfully. "I'm glad you like my pajamas! But what's wrong?"

David looked at her, searching her face for a hint of open-mindedness that would accept what he had just been through, accept what he had seen. He put his arm around Lisbeth's shoulder and pulled her closer to him. "I have to figure out a way to tell you," he said. "This is not an easy one."

Lisbeth sat straight up. "David what's wrong?"

"I promise I'll tell you when I can, when I find the words."

"Is it something to do with Bob and his nonsense? Did he give you any trouble?"

"Ha! Bob's been involved with two women. Not one, but two?"

"What?!"

"One of them's really young looking and very white. The other is also white and lives in their building," David said. He was hoping this line of conversation would distract Lisbeth so he wouldn't have to tell her what the real issue was. "…and you know how Kevin can be."

"I know. Did he hurt Bob?"

David smiled and said, "A little. Enough to scare him." David paused for a second. "Bob's got some real issues. He's confused as hell. Said he wants a wife like his partners have."

"What? What did he mean?"

"I'll tell you what he said, and then the very white girl will make sense. He said he wanted a white wife. Cath is too black for him. He's been involved with one of these women for three years. It's a hot mess."

"Oh my God." Lisbeth paused and studied David's face. Silence fell over them like a prayer shawl. A good minute passed. Lisbeth curled up into David's arms. "David?"

"Hmm?"

"That's not it, is it? Something else happened and don't bother to lie. I know you too well."

He smiled, kissed her hand and said, "Sweetheart, just give me some time. I need to digest it all. You know I can't keep anything from you for very long."

"Okay." Lisbeth paused before speaking again. "You want something to eat?"

"What I need is a drink, and then something to eat. Just a sandwich, something simple."

"Okay, you make your drink. I can do better than a sandwich." Lisbeth quietly walked down the hall to the kitchen. She was frowning, lost in thought. The only time David drank was when he lost a case, and he rarely lost a case. Lisbeth knew that whatever David was struggling with, it had to be big.

It was almost 2 A.M. by the time Lisbeth and David went to bed. Lisbeth told him about her day. She was a surgical nurse. Stupid doctors, crazy patients, not to mention the ineptitude of hospital administrators! She decided not to dwell on that and simply told David about the kids' activities.

By the time they turned off the bedroom lights, Lisbeth was ready to sleep. She drifted off quickly. But David was wide awake. His mind wandered around the valley of the impossible. How do you hold the impossible? He didn't know. But he knew Victoria was at the center of it and has been since she was born. There was so much he didn't understand, and so much that made him want to drink himself into oblivion. He convinced himself he didn't have to figure everything out right then! Finally, he fell asleep.

Thirty minutes later, David's eyes flipped open and found the room flooded with bright, white light. He heard a low-key consistent buzzing noise. David was confused and alarmed.

"What the hell is this?" he thought. He blinked his eyes,

trying to adjust to the bright light. Lisbeth was sound asleep. As his eyes adjusted, he found himself looking into this pool of blackness, the eyes of those Beings he encountered earlier. Their eyes seemed to speak a silent language of their own that mesmerized him. As they came closer and closer, David realized he couldn't move. He tried to scream and he couldn't. Lisbeth was somehow still sleeping through this. A strange sensation went through his body as if he was no longer a solid mass but something akin to electrical currents. And that description wasn't quite right either, but it was as close as he could come. Had they figured out a way to manipulate our molecular structure? Was that what was happening as his feet and legs went through the bedroom wall? Or did it have something to do with the electromagnetic force humans generate? Does each one of us have a unique electromagnetic signature? David didn't know. He was more than halfway through the wall by now, terrified of what would happen to his brain.

The harshness of the alarm screamed into David's ear. His arm flew out from underneath the covers and turned it off. David realized he had a headache. He rarely had headaches. Maybe it was the drink he had last night. Maybe it was the thought of Bob! Lisbeth started to wake up, groggy and a little disoriented.

She turned on her side and gazed at David, "Good morning," she whispered.

"How'd you sleep, babe?" he asked Lisbeth.

"You know, it was a deep sleep. Been a long time since I've slept like that," she said.

"You okay?" David asked.

"Oh, yeah. I'll shake it off. Let me take a shower. I'll be

okay." Lisbeth sat up on her side of the bed staring into space. "You know, I did have a crazy dream."

"How crazy?"

Lisbeth shook her head and laughed a little. She turned and looked at her husband. "Large insects with large black eyes! And there was a huge owl! What is that?"

"I don't know, babe. Anything happen or just the owl and insects?"

"It's weird. We were in an operating room – I think. Strange. Maybe it was something from work. Who knows!"

"I'll get the kids up," David said. "Go, take your shower. Put the insects and the owl on hold."

She dragged herself to the bathroom and closed the door. The minute the door clicked shut, David shot out from underneath the covers, stood, and realized his pajama bottoms were on backwards, and the top was unevenly buttoned. A few drops of blood screamed bright red on his light blue pajama top. He had no idea how this happened. That's what David told himself. But the more he thought about it, his knees gave way and he dropped onto his bed. He took some deep breaths, put his pajama bottoms on correctly, grabbed his robe from the foot of the bed and put it on quickly.

"What is going on?" David muttered. His head fell into his hands. He took another deep breath and heard himself say, "Did they take Lisbeth too, the kids? Dear God, walk with me. I don't know what the hell is going on."

CHAPTER FOURTEEN
Catherine Gets Help

"The only reason I'm here is because Sidney made me promise to see you. Sidney's my best friend. I'm not her best friend, but she's mine. Since prep school. Look, that's just the way it is. I'm just tellin' you. I wish I'd never told Sidney, but she figured it out anyway. Who am I kidding, right? The bruises couldn't be completely covered, although I tried. I thought being dark skinned... I don't know why I never heard anything from my mother. Maybe she did know and just never said anything... I mean I did see her after Bob hit me. What? Why would she do that? Because that's the way my mother is. She lives in an elaborate world of denial. She doesn't like something, she just pretends it's not there, until she can't. But somebody said something 'cause Kevin and David knew, and if Kevin and David knew, my mother knew.

"They're my brothers. David's my older brother and Kevin is the baby. I'm in the middle. What? Well it's tricky. David is a defense attorney and a good one. Yes, David Stockard, the litigator! Yes, he is something, always has been. They don't call him Johnnie Cochran East for nothing! And Kevin? He's the good-looking baby. He's an investment banker, takes after Dad's side of the family. He's lighter than David, lighter than me. David and I take after Mom and her people. What? You didn't really ask me that, did you? Why is skin color important in America? Have you been living under a rock for most of your life? C'mon.

"Anyway, listen, you can't get away with much having them for brothers. No, I don't feel overshadowed. Puh-leese.

I'm a college professor. I have tenure. Columbia University. Political Science. Sometimes, yeah, sometimes I'm a guest on MSNBC. You've seen me? Oh. Wow.

"Yes, I come from a smart family. My parents went to college and grad school and all of us did. Stupidity was not allowed. My father went to Morehouse, and David went there also. Then David went to Harvard Law. Kevin went to Harvard undergrad and the B School there. I got my PhD from Harvard and did undergraduate work there. What? Radcliffe was swallowed by the university. My parents were born in Alabama. My mother went to Fisk. Unusual? You think we're unusual? Why am I laughing? I'm laughing at you! How many black people do you know? It's Sidney who's unusual. Why? She's…a citizen of the world. Comfortable anywhere with anyone, and she's little, and scary smart. Maybe that's why she and my daughter get along. What does Sid do? Whatever she wants to! She's got some interesting abilities and credentials. We need to leave it at that, okay?

"I know. I know. Okay - Bob. What? When did it start? Long before anybody knew. Now that I think about it, everything started to go south when I was pregnant with Victoria. He got this asinine notion that Victoria wasn't his. As if I would have time for an affair! Then when she was born, he flipped out because Victoria didn't look like anybody in our families. Then we found out she's a genius. Bob could hardly stand it.

"Sidney mentioned Victoria to you? Well… Yes, she's a genius. What? The East Side School for Girls. Are you okay? You look funny… Unusual abilities? I guess. Victoria's not the problem. Bob and I are the problem. What? Bob is flat out hostile.

"Shortly after she was born, he started with verbal slams in private and then in public. He went out of his way to do that at his office parties. What? He's a lawyer, a partner, became a partner six, seven years ago. I think it's about resentment. I think he resents me paying for his last year and a half of law school. That and my PhD, and the offer I got from MSNBC. They want me to appear as a regular. Yeah. Thank you. Resentment. Jealousy. Maybe he's just a fool. I don't know.

"Money complicates things. It can be the third rail of any relationship. I mean…I think he didn't know how to handle me paying for his last year or so of law school. I don't know what happened. My family tried to talk me out of doing it… How? How what? My brother is an investment banker. We know money. We understand how to make it grow. When I first met Bob, I thought he was smart, kind. He seemed genuinely interested in me and didn't get put off by my credentials or upbringing. What? He grew up in the projects. His father vanished when he was five or six, and his mother had some addiction issues. I just think…

"What do you mean, how do I feel? Well, how do you think I should feel?! Why is it white women are always looking for somebody to cry? Crying…you guys cry at the drop of a hat and the friggin' world has to come to a stop! We cry and we have to keep going. What do you think would've happened had some of my female ancestors cried as slaves, while picking cotton, while working from can't see in the morning to can't see at night? Hostile? You think this is hostile? Umph! Don't ever expect me to come in here and cry – ever. What? You need to get over that strong black woman thing because you don't know the half of it – and if we're going to work together you've got some learning to do. Would I feel better with a black therapist? And what would I tell Sidney? No…it's you and me, Doctor. It's just that simple.

"You want to explore my feelings? Well, explore this; I don't ever want to see Robert Pittman again and I feel like shit! What?! See, damn it, I told Sid this wouldn't work. What do you mean, sit down? I can stand if I want to. Is that against the rules? Okay…I'll sit when I'm ready to sit. No, I don't need some water. I'm fine.

"The verbal abuse started when he made partner – and then roughly a year or two after he made partner, he started slapping me, then punching me. He did hit me when I was carrying Victoria. Yeah, that was before he made partner. She's twelve…going on 40! Anyway, it was usually after some office event, you know, staff outings, Christmas parties, or after some faculty gathering I had to attend. I stopped inviting him to faculty events. The idea of going out and then coming home to get slapped around was not something I wanted to experience. Yeah, I said that. He punched me when I was pregnant with Victoria. Where? Why is that important? No, I'm not hiding anything. He, well…first he slapped my face and then…my abdomen. It was… it was like he abused her before she was even born. I still wonder if she has some memory of that, but I guess not, right? He only did it once, maybe twice. What? Oh, I was pretty far along… five or six months. I found out that Christopher saw it all. He was just a little boy…and he didn't understand…

"I told Bob that Christopher saw him and I thought Bob

would stop, and he did for a while. After Victoria was born, he seemed to be on cloud nine for a few months and then, you know, she began to really develop her own features. She was no longer a generic, cute baby girl. She looked like somebody else's child. And something else happened. What? I don't know. Well…I'm just thinking…It had something to do with Stephan. Steph and Bob met when they went to City College. They became good friends. We owe Stephan a lot. If it wasn't for him, we would've never been accepted by the Condo Association. Steph had a meeting with them. I don't know what he said, but the next thing we knew, everything was fine. That's when I first met him. What? The man is the embodiment of everything masculinity should be about, physically, emotionally, socially, and a brainiac to boot!

"Hmm? No, he died almost a year ago. That's right. That Adam Stephan Aldrich. He preferred Stephan. Yes, that Sidney Barrett, the artist, my friend. She referred me to you, so she knows you! Anyway – Stephan was a big deal, a real sweetheart…and very good looking for a white boy…and not just any white boy! You can believe what you read. He was an extraordinary human being. He's really comfortable around black folks, you know. He came from a family with very deep pockets that held not just old money but ancient money! But what a wonderful man he was. Down to earth, kind…a little tight with a dollar but that's okay… Yeah, he really was all that. I'm sure he had faults. You'd have to talk to Sidney about that. My daughter loved him… So did my son. I think I'll have some water now.

"Victoria had a crush on Stephan from day one! After I got home from the hospital, I remember him coming by to visit, and I let him hold her. Her big eyes just latched on to him and that was it. When she got old enough to walk, she would run to him when he came by. Stephan loved children. He loved babies. And Christopher thought Stephan was one cool dude. What? No, Bob didn't like that. Christopher was his son. What can I say? Both of our kids loved Stephan and Bob couldn't compete with him. In Bob's mind, Stephan came to represent everything Bob wanted to be and couldn't be – and Stephan and Sid got married... I don't know something snapped in Bob.

"What? Well, I told you Victoria is smarter than all of us! She's been at the East Side School for Girls since the first grade. Yes, that school! I know their reputation. Look Victoria can read a book in a few hours and comprehend everything in it. And I don't mean Dick & Jane. I'm talking about authors like Virginia Wolf, Jane Austen, George Sands. I read those authors in college! She's studying Farsi. I don't know how she knows what she knows half the time. Honestly, there're times when she doesn't feel like my daughter. I haven't figured that out yet... But Christopher is definitely my son! If I were a boy, I'd be like Christopher. I don't know why Bob ... Bob just stopped paying attention to Chris... Bob is... He keeps saying Victoria isn't his. I don't understand.

"What did you say? A hybrid... A hybrid of what?! Oh, come on! Really? You see a lot of parents from Vic's school? Why? I cannot believe that. Hybrid children. You just said that... How? What? Human and alien? As in outer space?! No. That's absurd.

"Listen to me. I cannot accommodate that thought much less the possibility of that. I won't talk about it. No. My life is not an episode on *Star Trek*. Anyway, that's impossible. I don't care what you think.

"What? What do you mean, why didn't I leave him? Look – and Sid asked me the same damned thing – I am not like Sid. I need a husband in my life and for my children. You don't understand... The proudest day in my mother's life was when I got married, even though she couldn't stand Bob. Yes! The Ph.D., the MSNBC deal? No. The fact that I eventually got an M.R.S. degree was my mother's crowning moment. Look Doctor, I could've gotten the Nobel Peace Prize and that would've meant nothing to her if I wasn't married. What? My father thought I was too good for any man, and he couldn't stand Bob. Dad considered Bob trash because of his background, his family or lack thereof. Truth be told, my mother had David do a background check on Bob – and when my parents found out a couple of years ago that he took the kids to meet his cousin or somebody who lived in the projects... Well that was it. The kids were scared half to death when they came home. My father found out, called Bob, and demanded an explanation. Why was he exposing his grandchildren to 'that element' of life? That was my father's question. It was a mess. My father died roughly two years ago. Bob didn't lose any sleep over it. He hated my father. He resented Stephan. He's suspicious of Sidney, and I'm not good enough for him anymore. Why? Don't you get it? I'm too dark, too big. I'm not dainty. I don't have good hair. I speak my mind. I'm not white! He decided that he needed a white wife to match his partnership expectations. Hell, I don't care if I ever see him again. David put me in touch with a divorce attorney. We have an appointment at the end of the week.

"So, Doctor, tell me, what is it we're going to do here? Fix my self-esteem? My what? A new life? Who said I needed a new life? I've got my family, my kids, my students. I've got Sid and my work. What? Well you keep asking questions about her! Look, Sidney is the closest thing I have to a sister. Okay? That's just the way it is.

"I have to take care of my kids. You know, Christopher got in a fist fight with his father right after Steph died. I don't know. Bob used to play basketball with Christopher every Saturday morning for years, and then he just stopped. Who stepped in? Steph. He took Chris to his gym every week to play basketball until he died. What? The fight? Oh. Christopher won. Knocked Bob off his feet. It was ugly, very demeaning for Bob. He had two broken ribs. That was a real turning point. Where did it happen? At the condo. I told you right after Steph died. When? The day after. What do I think it was about? Christopher is very protective of me. Victoria saw it all. When I got home, she was terrified and had locked herself in her bedroom. Me? I was out buying groceries. Bob told me what happened. He was so humiliated. It was never the same between him and Christopher. I don't know. Victoria…I didn't know how to make her feel safe, but Stephan did. She started spending more and more time with Sidney and Steph. Cope? Me? How? I drink, Doctor. I drink. So, Madam Shrink, what's your recommendation?

"Twice a week? Are you serious? The kids too! What? Family therapy for all of us, and individual therapy for me? Do I look like an ATM machine?"

PART TWO
Father & Daughter

CHAPTER FIFTEEN
Catherine Gets More Help

Catherine walked to Dr. Hudson's office deep in thought a week after their first session. "Hudson's nuts. Victoria, a hybrid? I can't even put my head around that. Hmph! Maybe Bob..." Catherine walked into the waiting room and flopped down in a chair. She looked around noting some high-end prints, a large, healthy, Ficus plant, and this little thing that sat on the floor and generated white noise, making it impossible to hear what was going on inside Hudson's office. There was a different door clients used to leave when their session was over. "Very clever," Catherine thought. "You don't want to run into anybody you know coming out of here!"

Hudson opened her office door. She was a striking woman with very dark eyes that went right through you. Her hands were unusually beautiful like Claire Butterfield's hands. For some reason, it made Catherine nervous.

"Catherine, come in," she said. "I'm glad you came back."

Catherine got up. It was as if she had lead weights on each shoulder. Drinking a glass of Clorox was more appealing to Catherine than spending the next "50 minute hour" with Hudson.

After hanging up her coat, Catherine sat down opposite of Hudson into a comfortable, upholstered chair, and waited.

"Victoria? She's great."

"Tell me all the things you are in relation to Victoria," Hudson said.

"I'm her mother. What else would I be? What is Sidney?

What kind of question is that? Sidney's like her fairy Godmother. Her favorite Aunt who spoils her rotten. Look, Sidney is Victoria and Christopher's guardian if something should happen to me or Bob. Why? Because that's the way Victoria wanted it! You know, Dr. Hudson I really don't want to talk about it if you're going to... Investigate what? What am I supposed to tell you? She reads college level books. She's got a gift for languages. She helps Chris with his homework! I can discuss politics with her. She's twelve! Vic has all kinds of questions but you know something, she also watches people. I mean, really watches people. It's like she's looking right through you. Say what? I thought I made it clear I didn't want to talk about that. Are you telling me you believe in aliens? Who really needs help here?! Okay, okay. Go ahead. I'll try to answer the best I can. Yes, I've seen her do extraordinary things. Like what? I'm thinking. She knows how to revive dying plants. I've seen her move things without touching them. No. There's more... I was walking by her bedroom and the door was half open. She was sitting on the floor, cross legged, staring into space. No, she wasn't daydreaming. I could tell by the look on her face. She was looking at something I couldn't see because... What? Give me a minute. Slowly, this tiny chair materialized. It was suspended in air. She moved her head down and the chair went down until it was on the floor. What? I don't know. It scared me. Tiny chairs today, what is it tomorrow?"

Hudson had a very quiet demeanor. She waited before asking the next question, knowing the profundity of it.

"What? A host... Dr. Hudson, who the hell are you? What

is it you're trying to tell me in this roundabout way? No. The government? Okay, Dr. Hudson, we have to stop. I can't take any more. Under ordinary circumstances I'm a fairly sophisticated person, not compared to Sidney, but it is what it is. Prepared for what?! And you want to know why I drink? Wouldn't you drink? Dr. Hudson, I need a straight answer, who the hell are you and what relationship do you have to the East Side School for Girls? Never mind me. Why is the government so interested in my daughter? Say what? What the hell do you mean, she's going to need to be with her own kind? Her parents!? What are you telling me? I can't believe any of this. Why? I don't want to believe it. I can't.

CHAPTER SIXTEEN
A Note From Vic...

I like where Uncle David lives. It's quiet and very beautiful. I think I'd like to live there if I couldn't stay with Aunt Sidney. I'd like to live anywhere without my parents. I wish I could just visit my mother – not live with her – because she can't really take care of us. I mean, if Christopher's around I'd be okay. But Mom can't protect me from Dad. It's like she doesn't even see me half the time. If she doesn't see me, how can she miss me? How would she know I wasn't around?

A week before we all moved in with Aunt Sidney, Dad tied me up and locked me in his den closet again while Mom was in the kitchen. I tried to fight him off, but he grabbed me and put some duct tape over my mouth, then tied me up like I was some kind of farm animal. I got so mad and scared I couldn't do anything! If Chris hadn't noticed I was gone I might've suffocated in that closet. I heard Chris ask, where was I and Mom said, "I don't know. Check her room." Chris said he did and I was gone. Then Mom told him she had to read some papers from her students and to ask Dad. I heard Chris walk into the den. Then everything went silent for a minute and I started to cry. That's when I saw Uncle Stephan. He just appeared in the closet. It was like he was real, alive, not dead at all. He told me everything was going to be okay, that I'd be fine, that Christopher would find me and take me to Aunt Sidney's house.

Then I heard a loud thump and Chris asking Dad what he did with me. He mumbled something and I heard another thump and then somebody got hit. The next thing I knew, the closet door opened. It was Chris. He untied me and removed the tape Dad put over my mouth.

Chris picked me up and said, "C'mon. I've got to get you out of here." He took me to my room. Chris was scared. I was scared. He looked at my face and asked if Dad had hit me, if I was hurt. I lied. I told him no. Dad locked me in the closet because he didn't want to see me. Chris told me to pack some things while he called Aunt Sidney. She was mad when Chris told her!!

He got my jacket from the hall closet. Mom was in the breakfast room reading papers. She heard everything! She was pretending she didn't hear anything. How could she not hear anything? What's wrong with grown-ups? Dad came out of the den. I knew he wanted to say something but he saw Chris and stopped. I was at the front door when Chris told him, "You lay a hand on my little sister again and I will break every bone in your body and everybody will know why." I'm never going back to the condo. When Aunt Sidney called Mom, Mom pretended she didn't know anything about it and told me to come home. I refused and spent the week with Aunt Sidney. When I went home, it was crazy and now we're all staying with Aunt Sidney.

Dad should die. Something has to be done about him. I hate him. I have to find a new father. Pretty soon I'm going to hate my mother also. I don't like her and I don't want to be like her either. I want to be like Aunt Sidney. I hope they don't screw things up with Mr. Solomon. I'm going to his school whether they like it or not!

CHAPTER SEVENTEEN
Butterfield & Solomon

Catherine was seated outside of Claire Butterfield's office. She's the headmistress of this fancy, private school on the upper East Side of Manhattan. The school had been a private residence of some ridiculously wealthy New Yorker from the nineteenth century who died and wanted a private girl's school to be established there. It was simply known as The East Side School for Girls, grades one through eight. The school was progressive yet disciplined. Entrance exams were required and it helped if the student's family was college educated and professional.

Victoria was one of ten children of color in the school population of two hundred. This was a second home to her. Faculty and administrators knew the children in ways most of their parents didn't. The East Side School for Girls was exclusive in mysterious ways as were most of the students and all of the faculty. No one really understood how the entrance exams were used. Your child had to be gifted in some unusual way that the school determined. These children were abnormally bright, intelligent, intense, and focused in ways you didn't expect from someone until college or beyond. Regardless of their age, they were all petite, but physically strong. The students' work created new paradigms that generated new expectations and possibilities. These little girls have a combination of maturity and precociousness that could easily drive parents crazy or intimidate them! Every one of these tiny geniuses would grow up and make a difference in the world. That was not only a given, but an expectation.

The faculty had international credentials: the London School of Economics, the Sorbonne, schools in India and Japan that were unheard of in the United States. Others were working scientists investigating artificial intelligence, bionic replacements for human limbs and organs, the survival of consciousness after death and the definition of death. These faculty members had a worldly air about them, sophisticated and highly focused on the students. The administrators were also educators and their backgrounds revealed work with many government agencies. They had titles of responsibility that were diplomatically vague. The title that kept popping up all the time was Special Assistant, Special Assistant at the CIA, at the FBI, at the NSC, to the President of the United States.

There was an aura of refinement and confidentiality about the school that no one could fully articulate but feel. Very few students were accepted. The public, including the parents of the girls, were never told exactly why their children made the grade. Only the faculty and Ms. Butterfield saw the exam results.

The curriculum included annual trips to the American Ballet, Alvin Ailey, the Museum of Modern Art, visiting artists' studios, watching surgeries in teaching hospitals, talking with judges, visiting Congress, being invited to NASA, observing trials, and talking with scientists in a variety of fields. The arts and sciences were equals at the school. There were art classes and mandatory instructions in chess, introductions to Freud, Jung and Fromm in the seventh and eighth grades. Students were taught the history of the world with equal emphasis, and in the first grade they were immersed in a foreign language of their choice. French,

Spanish, Russian, Farsi, Mandarin Chinese and Japanese were offered. By the time they graduated, students would be completely fluent in at least one if not two languages in addition to English. Victoria chose Farsi. By the age of twelve, Victoria understood the social, political, and environmental significance of the Middle East. Students were taught that language(s) reflected their culture. If you wanted to understand the culture of a people it would be reflected in their language.

Victoria had also been taught that it was important to communicate with people in their own language to better understand how they think. Why she chose Farsi in the first grade no one knew.

By the sixth grade, Victoria and her classmates were shaped and trained to think differently. They created new forms of human intelligence and different values. This kind of education allowed students to more readily accept the global nature of the problems we face with technology connecting everyone in a matter of minutes, regardless. Charles Solomon and his associates were creating a generation that would not only be adept at thinking differently but would meet whatever the future delivered for better or worse, to survive and lead. Victoria was one of the brightest members of her generation.

Seated outside of Claire Butterfield's office, Catherine was overwhelmed by the potential and mystery of her daughter. A guard stood directly across from Ms. Butterfield's door. Did he have a gun? He had an earpiece and one of those devices peeking out discretely at the cuff of his shirt sleeve that the Secret Service use to talk to each other. Why? Who would he be talking to, wondered Catherine? She felt a chill run down her body and back up through her head.

The guard was solidly built. A dark suit with an off-white shirt, a blue tie, and sensible black shoes. His face was motionless. His eyes missed nothing. Thinking about the gun he must have on him made Catherine clench her jaw. Standing ten to fifteen feet to the left of Catherine was a female security person that reminded Catherine of Peter Pan. She was tiny and wispy with a pixie haircut, an image that faded when Catherine got a glimpse of the gun holster poorly hidden by her suit jacket. Maybe it was supposed to be seen.

Lumbering down the hall, huffing and puffing, his coat open, a briefcase in one hand, Bob approached Catherine. The guard's eyes latched onto Bob.

"Catherine?"

Jolted from thinking about her daughter and this school, Catherine looked up and said, "Oh… I didn't see you…"

"I want to talk to you about your brothers," Bob said.

"Don't start, Bob. Not here, please." Both security people studied Bob. Their eyes never left him. He sat next to Catherine. She inched away from him, something the male guard noted.

Ms. Butterfield opened her office door, "Mr. and Mrs. Pittman. I'm so glad you're here. Please come in."

Bob strode in, a frown defining his face, followed by Catherine. Looking at Ms. Butterfield, Catherine thought she didn't look like a head mistress. She had an air about her that made you think of words like guardian, cultivator, and mentor. Well dressed, nails manicured, flawless cream-colored skin, she moved with grace. Her dark shoulder length hair glistened. There was nothing academic about Ms. Butterfield. She depressed Catherine. Ms. Butterfield was attractive in ways Catherine could never match. Ms. Butterfield was white and had straight hair. Catherine's mother made it clear when she was growing up that dark-skinned black women with thick, kinky hair were never considered pretty, much less attractive. So, it was important to be smart in case nobody wanted to marry you. Catherine made sure she was smart and was making sure Victoria was also, just in case, as if Victoria needed encouragement to be smart or intelligent!

Bob sat in a chair next to Catherine. Ms. Butterfield nodded at the security guard and thanked him. He left the room and took his position right outside her office door. It wasn't the first time Catherine had been in Ms. Butterfield's office. It was sleek, classy, neat! On one wall was an original Rothko. "My God," Catherine thought. "How many tuitions have paid for that?!" Catherine suddenly realized there was someone else in the room seated in the corner on the couch that defined one end of Ms. Butterfield's office.

Uneasy, Bob noticed him also. He stared at this person for a moment and then focused on Ms. Butterfield who was now seated behind her desk.

"Mr. and Mrs. Pittman, please, make yourselves comfortable," Ms. Butterfield said. "Can I get you some tea, coffee?"

"No thank you," Catherine said. She took off her coat and sat down.

"I'm good," Bob mumbled. He didn't take off his coat. He sat like a statue in the chair next to Catherine. Butterfield watched Bob with owl-like eyes.

"Very good," Ms. Butterfield said. "I'd like you to meet my colleague, Charles Solomon, founder of the Solomon School for Girls. Charles?"

Rising like smoke from some ancient ritual, Charles Solomon stood. His presence completely filled the room. He was tall, with an air of gravitas, beautifully dressed, and unnervingly attractive in ways that defied articulation. He could've been forty-five or sixty-five! And then there were his eyes, two bottomless, still pools of blackness. Catherine found him magnetic. She couldn't shake the feeling. He made Bob very nervous. Charles Solomon was the man who stood in the living room corner of Bob and Catherine's condo when Bob was moving out. This was the man who vanished like smoke.

CHAPTER EIGHTEEN
A Father's Love

Charles Solomon sat in a chair next to Claire Butterfield's desk facing Bob and Catherine. Ms. Butterfield never took her eyes off of the Pittmans. Bob looked into her dark eyes and swallowed hard. Little beads of perspiration started to spread across his forehead.

"Mr. Pittman, are you all right? Can I get you something? You're not looking very well right now," Ms. Butterfield said.

"No," he whispered. Looking at Solomon, Bob said, "You just… somehow you're familiar. That's all. I'm fine." Bob took a deep breath and then blew it out.

Solomon smiled before saying anything. "Mr. and Mrs. Pittman, Thank you for coming in today. I want to talk to you about Victoria," Solomon said. His voice had the undercurrent of a foreign accent that couldn't be placed. His warm smile calmed Catherine and alarmed Bob.

"Is there something wrong with Victoria?" Catherine asked trying not to stare at him. Solomon exuded power, strength and depth. Every time he breathed, Catherine felt he was embracing her, not romantically, but protectively. It was dizzy making.

"No, no, quite the contrary. I know you realize Victoria's very intelligent. Otherwise she wouldn't be here. Your daughter is beyond intelligent. She has a unique gift, several unique gifts to be accurate."

Clearing his throat, Bob asked, "What do you mean? Like art? Reading?"

Mr. Solomon's smile faded. Focusing directly on Bob,

Solomon said, "No. She has a remarkable ability for executive thinking."

"What does that mean?" Bob asked while he bounced his knee up and down before he felt a force stop it. Solomon was staring at Bob's knee.

"I think I know what it means," Catherine said. "Something to do with analysis and strategic thinking, organizing."

"Yes, that's close, Mrs. Pittman. But Victoria's capacity exceeds measurement."

Silence drenched the room. It was the phrase exceeds measurement that grabbed Bob and Catherine. "How did you find out? Is there some sort of test?" Catherine asked.

Solomon laughed. "Mrs. Pittman, you don't have a test for Victoria! We, or rather, Claire stumbled upon it," he said while nodding toward Ms. Butterfield.

Shifting in his seat, Bob asked while looking at his watch, "So what does this mean? You give her more homework? Do we get some tutors for her? What? I mean, what's so special about being able to organize, analyze…"

Charles Solomon's cordial demeanor and smile faded. He glared at Bob. Turning to Ms. Butterfield, Solomon said, "Perhaps you should tell them."

Ms. Butterfield stared at Bob before starting. "This is what made me call Mr. Solomon. Last year…"

Bob interrupted and said, "Last year? You've been knowing this for a year and now you're calling us?" He looked down at his watch again.

"Mr. Pittman, do you have some other place to be?" The chill in Solomon's voice terrified Catherine. Solomon was studying Bob and came to the final conclusion that Bob would have to be removed.

"No, I'm good… for a little bit," Bob said.

"Mr. Pittman," Ms. Butterfield said. "Please let me finish. Victoria can design wars. Her strategic reasoning is extraordinary. Don't let her size or demeanor fool you. She also has a gift for language. She reads on an adult level. She can reason way beyond her years. And, she has several psychic abilities. All of these capabilities need to be carefully cultivated."

"This is something to be excited over?" Bob asked. "I don't believe a word of it. Next thing you'll be telling me is she can move things without touching them! It's a trick. That's all it is. I've seen her do that and it's nothing but a cheap magic trick!" Hush fell in the room, like dark storm clouds approaching from the horizon.

Catherine shot him a look that hissed, "Shut up."

"I detect some contempt in your voice regarding Victoria," Solomon said. "Are you having a problem with her?"

Catherine answered too quickly and said, "No, not at all."

Bob said, "She's a freak. Victoria is abnormal. I'm just putting it out there. No need to soft pedal it."

"All the more reason she should come to the Solomon School," Ms. Butterfield said. "There she will be treasured. Correct Charles?"

"I already treasure her," Solomon said.

The room filled with Solomon's silence as he glared at Bob. It was palpable. "Ms. Butterfield knows what to look for in special children," Solomon said. "She called me immediately when she recognized the depth and extent of Victoria's skills. I flew up from Washington and I talked with Victoria. I also gave her six problems to solve. I'm not talking about arithmetic, Mr. Pittman. These problems were modified for her, problems based on CIA cases, the War College, the State Department, and the behavioral unit of the FBI. Do you understand? Your daughter, Mr. Pittman, at twelve years old, has a mind perfect for military, strategic planning."

Bob swallowed hard. Catherine's eyes welled up slightly with tears. She grabbed her stomach. "Wait until Dr. Hudson hears this," Catherine thought.

"Victoria has the capacity to solve these kinds of problems. I gave her three related to several upcoming emergencies this planet will experience unless something's done to turn it around. That's when I realized we were incapable of measuring her capacity in traditional ways," Solomon said staring at Bob. "Victoria and I have conversations about the moral implications of her gifts. This kind of genius is rare among your kind. It can go either way. I want to make sure her genius is developed to do good."

"What do you mean by 'your kind'? Are you saying that because she's Black and you don't think Black people are smart?" Bob asked.

Solomon sighed, "No that's not what I'm saying at all."

"Then what are you saying?"

"Mr. Pittman, there are no other human children that we've found like her. If there are, we don't know about it. Victoria is a rare gift…to the universe." Solomon gave Bob a look that resembled lightning. "Mr. Pittman, don't you love your daughter? She may be different but quite loveable. I love her. Why can't you?"

There was silence. Bob ignored Solomon. Catherine

started to bite her lower lip. She sensed there was a secret hanging in the air but she didn't want to know what it was. She ignored that phrase, human children. What other kind of children could there be?

"So, what do you want us to do?" Catherine asked trying not to show her alarm at the implications of what Solomon asked.

"Let her stay here and finish the sixth grade with her class. Developing social skills is important for these children. From time to time, I will come up and work with Victoria for a few days. When she finishes this year, we'll take care of everything. By the way, it would be very helpful if I could meet the rest of your family."

"Whoa. We? Who are you?" Bob asked.

Solomon looked at Butterfield and she tried not to roll her eyes. She composed herself and said, "Charles runs a very special school outside of Washington, DC, in northern Virginia for uniquely gifted children. The faculty and staff there see to it that the students develop their skills, refine their intelligence, and prepare them for the world that's forming right around us at speeds we can hardly keep up with."

"What does this special school cost?" Bob asked.

"There is no cost to you. The school and the cost for educating all of them is underwritten by a half dozen philanthropists from all over," Solomon said. They all sat in silence again for several seconds.

"Mr. Solomon," Catherine said, "What if we don't want Victoria to be part of this? What if we want her to grow up like any other little girl?"

Solomon stared at Catherine with a kind of knowing that

terrified her. He reached in his jacket pocket and pulled out a card. "Mrs. Pittman, show this card to you brother, David. See what he thinks. My phone number is on the card. Call me when you talk with David. I'm hoping you will see not only the advantages in all this, but the wisdom behind it. The older Victoria gets, the more difficult it's going to be for her to fit in with average children and teens her own age. Trust me, Victoria already knows she's not like other children. She knows her destiny."

Looking at his watch, Bob stood and said, "Look, I have to go. I've got a new client and I have to get back… Mr. Solomon…" Bob extended his hand to Solomon.

Solomon rose and shook Bob's hand. "You be careful with that new client. All that glitters isn't gold, you know. Derrick Graham could be problematical for you."

How did Solomon know this? Bob was speechless, so much so that he didn't notice Solomon's hand felt like stainless steel.

"I'm hoping you and Mrs. Pittman will take advantage of this opportunity for Victoria's sake. I would hate for it to be any other way. We've loved her from the moment she stepped in here at six years old. We've nurtured her, or rather Ms. Butterfield has. We have given Victoria what you have been incapable of. We're ready to take over now."

Bob glared at Solomon and asked, "How do you know about Derrick Graham? How do you know?" Bob was afraid in a way he had never experienced before. He wanted to run. Solomon knew too much and Bob felt naked, defenseless, and he didn't like it.

Charles Solomon smiled at Bob before saying anything. "Mr. Pittman, we are very thorough when it comes to understanding the backgrounds of our students. We want to be able to anticipate and address any problems they may experience. It may sound old fashioned, but we're her parents also…" Solomon's look sent a sharp chill through Bob. He found himself shuddering.

Catherine stood and said. "Mr. Solomon, Thank you. I promise we will think carefully about your offer. I'm sure we'll come to some mutually satisfying agreement. Unless there's anything else we should know…"

"No Mrs. Pittman, I think you understand. Talk to Victoria. See how she feels," Solomon said. He smiled at Catherine again and for a second she wondered if he was flirting with her.

"I will, Mr. Solomon."

"Remember, I want to meet the rest of your family. By the way, I've seen you on MSNBC. You're brilliant and beautiful," Solomon said never taking his eyes off her.

Catherine smiled. "You're too kind. Ms. Butterfield, Thank you," Catherine said. Her heart was pounding. "How did Solomon know about David? What was he trying to tell Bob?" Catherine wondered. Too many questions flew through her head. "Who is Charles Solomon, really? What's the motive?" Catherine felt someone staring at her. She turned and saw Solomon looking at her. "Is there a problem, Mr. Solomon?"

"None at all, Mrs. Pittman. I was just thinking that you are an extraordinary looking woman. I hope you know that."

Caught off guard, Catherine's eyes widened. She smiled and thanked him again.

The security guard had already walked Bob out and put

him in a cab. By the time Catherine got to the main entrance, Bob was gone. In true New York fashion, Catherine stepped into the street and hailed a cab. The cab would be forced to stop or run her over! After she closed the cab door, she saw Butterfield and Solomon watching her leave.

As the cab pulled away, Solomon told Butterfield, "Mr. Pittman's a problem and so is she."

Hands clasped behind her back, Ms. Butterfield said, "He's always been a problem. He's destroying Mrs. Pittman and of course there's Victoria."

Solomon said, "We will take care of Mr. Pittman…soon, before he does any more damage. Victoria's strong and smart but she's still a little girl. She's had some close calls with him."

Catherine gave the driver explicit instructions to Columbia University preventing him from taking "the long way" and running up the fare. With that done, she pulled out her cell phone and called David on his private line. The phone rang once.

"Sis, what's up?" David said. The tone of his voice made her think of basketballs bouncing on a wooden court!

"David, I've got to talk to you." Catherine noticed she felt shaky and a little light-headed.

"Okay, I've got some time. Talk to me." David leaned back in his chair and took a sip of lukewarm coffee that had been sitting on his desk for almost a half hour.

She looked at the card and said, "David, do you know a Charles Solomon from Washington, D.C.? Have your paths crossed?" There was silence. "David?" He'd been doodling some of those big eyed, insect-like creatures on a napkin.

"Yeah, I know of him." David put his cup of coffee down

and started doodling again. "We've never had lunch or anything. He's well known in the intelligence community in D.C. You don't have to know him to understand his power and influence. Why?"

"He wants to work with Victoria, have her attend his school next year," Catherine said. "Bob and I just had the strangest meeting with him at Victoria's school, and he knows you, or at least he says he does."

David stopped doodling and sat up in his chair. "Solomon knows about everybody that's important for him to know. He probably knows what kind of toothpaste I use. Listen to me. If he says he wants to work with her, he's already working with Victoria. By the time they approach you it's a done deal. We need to talk but not on the phone. The fact that he mentioned me means he wants me to talk to you. Dinner tonight, sis. Trust me, you've only got forty-eight hours before you'll hear from him."

"I wasn't planning on cooking… We're still at Sid's. Maybe Sid can take the kids out and we can have her place. Would that work?" Catherine asked, concerned given the shift in the tone of David's voice.

"I hope so. You can't say no to this man, Cath. I gotta go. I'll be at Sid's around seven." David hung up and muttered to himself, "Lord Jesus!"

CHAPTER NINETEEN
Now It Gets Serious

David drove around the block three times before finding a parking space. He walked down the street to Sidney's brownstone. Sidney always managed to get a parking space in front of her house. He couldn't understand how that happened so consistently. Ringing the doorbell, David noticed a dark colored car parked directly opposite of Sidney's brownstone. He turned his head casually and saw a man seated behind the wheel of the car. At that moment, Sidney opened the door.

Hey," she said! "We've been waiting for you," Sidney said. "Come on in. It's cold out there."

David walked in, locked the door behind him, and hugged Sidney. "Girl, what's going on?" Bonwit and Coco charge from the living room towards them, barking with tails wagging.

"I don't know. You tell me. Everybody's downstairs. C'mon."

As they walked downstairs, with the spaniels leading, David grabbed her hand and whispered, "I think we're being watched."

Sidney's head whipped around and he put his forefinger on his lips and shook his head. She understood and continued down the stairs, showing no surprise or anxiety.

They walked in the kitchen and found Catherine, Victoria, and Christopher. "What's going on down here?" David asked rhetorically.

Victoria ran over and hugged her uncle. "Aunt Sidney's taking us out. The choices are Chinese, Italian or pizza."

Holding his niece, he kissed the top of her head and then looked at his nephew. "What's up my man? You too old and sophisticated to give your uncle a hug?"

Christopher grinned, and loped over to hug him. "Hey Uncle David."

"That's better. Baby sister, what's your excuse?" David started to walk towards her.

"God, David. You get more and more like Daddy every day," Catherine said as she strode over to hug her brother.

"That's not a bad thing, is it?" he asked. "It worked for Daddy."

All of them huddled around the kitchen island and decided where to go for dinner. Pizza won. The kids and Sidney got dressed and left saying they'd be back in an hour. David and Catherine settled in the living room. She sat next to him on the couch and he held her hand.

"Listen to me," he whispered.

"Why are you whispering?" she asked in a normal voice

David gave her a look he perfected in childhood when Catherine was on the verge of getting in trouble with one of their parents. His eyes fixed on her face in no uncertain terms.

Recognizing the look, she became serious and whispered back, "Whatever you say."

"I'm going to start talking in a normal voice and all you're going to say is I understand or I'll think about it. Lose the push back for now."

Catherine nodded her head and he let go of her hand.

"So, Charles Solomon. Quite a reputation among DC's intelligence communities. I did some research… Great opportunity for Victoria."

"Okay, I understand. I'll think about it," Catherine said. Her eyes were wide with concern. "David, I don't even know the name of the school. He glided in telling me very little, now that I think about it."

"It's The Solomon School for Girls… They've got a website."

"He's the founder? My God," exclaimed Catherine. "Where is the school?"

David stood. "I think it's in northern Virginia or somewhere in the Berkshires of Massachusetts. I'll tell you one thing though Bob better get with the program. If they perceive him as a problem, they'll remove him, do you understand?"

"I got it, David. I understand I think." Catherine was slightly dizzy. "David, what are we dealing with? What is going on?"

"Victoria's always been smart and if Solomon's interested that means we've got a unique brainiac among us."

"Look, I need a glass of wine. Can we go downstairs? The wine's in the dining room."

Catherine stood. A bit light-headed and dizzy, her body was stiff from tension. She stumbled a little but she made it down the stairs. David was close behind. After pouring a glass of wine, she walked in the kitchen, found a note pad and pencil, then scribbled, when can we really talk, and pushed it in front of David. He scribbled back, soon. Catherine rolled her eyes.

"Listen, we need to have a family meeting, without the kids," David said. "This is family business."

"What about Bob?" Catherine asked, frowning.

"He really needs to be there so I can explain the new facts

of life now," David said. "I'll work it out with the court so he can come."

"You're scaring me, David," Catherine said.

"That's a very sane and wise response. Sane and wise."

The spaniels started to bark. The sound of feet racing in the house startled David and Catherine. His eyes scanned the kitchen looking for something he could use as a weapon. Catherine froze.

"Uncle David, we've got pizza," screamed Victoria as she flew down the stairs and into the kitchen! Christopher followed her holding the large, white pizza box.

Exhaling, David said, "I thought you were going to eat out."

Sidney walked in with a troubled look on her face and said, "That was the plan."

Looking through the kitchen drawers for the pizza cutter, Victoria blurted out, "We couldn't be there. I think we were being watched."

Christopher found some plates, looked at his little sister and said, "You're such a little drama queen – no, a drama princess - sometimes. Why would anybody be watching us?"

"Christopher, I think your sister's right," Sidney said.

Everybody stopped. Victoria looked from face to face to face and said, "I don't think they were bad watchers. I think they were good watchers. They weren't going to hurt us."

David looked at Sidney for a response.

Sidney nodded then said, "I didn't sense any danger from them."

"Them! How many are we talking about?" Catherine demanded.

Slices of pizza were passed around. Victoria folded her slice, took a bite and announced, "Two, a man and a woman. I think I've seen the woman before. She's a security guard at school who looks like an elf!" Victoria finished her slice and reached for another, leaving the adults at a loss for words.

Christopher stared at the adults and his sister. "Something's up," he thought. "And it's serious."

It was Saturday, late morning. Lisbeth and David were in the kitchen drinking coffee. It was a week before Thanksgiving and getting colder with each passing day. The trees were free of any leaves and the days were growing shorter. Lisbeth suffered from seasonal affective disorder that kicked in when it started to get dark around 4:15 in the afternoon. On most days though she was at the hospital and rarely noticed the darkening of days except when she was off. She hated winter.

Maybe it would snow before Thanksgiving she thought. Lisbeth had a long list of things to do before the holidays. Just thinking about them made her weary. She looked tired but still younger than her forty-five years. Lisbeth was born looking serious. She didn't smile often. One reason she loved her husband was his ability to make her laugh.

"David, I don't know if I'm going to get through this holiday season," she said while putting three spoons of sugar in her coffee.

"You say that every year and every year we get through it with flying colors – and it's because of you!" He leaned over and kissed her on the cheek. "All the kids gone?"

"Every last one of them, thank God!" she said.

David laughed. "Have they been that bad this week?" He

poured himself another cup of coffee.

"Incorrigible! That's your third cup of coffee this morning. Try not to drink a fourth! What about Christopher and Victoria?" Lisbeth asked.

"They've got stuff to do on the weekends and then they go back to Sid's," David said.

David told his wife exactly who was coming for this family meeting. Lisbeth got along well with her husband's siblings, but his mother, Ruth, was a particular source of aggravation. Ruth was one of those mothers in laws who thought nobody was good enough for her children. Only half listening to David, Lisbeth remembered the first time she met Ruth. David's father, Matthew Pittman, was still alive then.

The four of them went out to dinner in Manhattan. Ruth found something wrong with the food and the service. David ignored his mother's complaints because she was critical of everything and the elder Pittman, Matthew, looked at his wife and said, "Enough Ruth." She stopped complaining and turned her attention to Lisbeth. Silently groaning, Lisbeth remembered that moment with brutal clarity.

Eyes narrowing, Ruth asked Lisbeth, "Where do you come from? Do you have any family? We're a very close family and all you young people today who just up and leave and don't think about anybody but themselves... I don't understand it and they're not brought up in the church..."

Matthew Pittman put his fork down and said, "Ruth, let the young lady talk. Do you really think David would introduce us to someone he's not comfortable with and doesn't reflect our values? If he's comfortable with her, we should be too."

"I'm not worried about David," Ruth said, then turned to look directly at Lisbeth. "It's Lisbeth. We don't know a thing about you Lisbeth, and David's taking us to this fancy restaurant where they can't cook with these waiters who obviously have no good home training, and for what?"

"Mom! Stop. I've invited you and Dad out tonight to tell you something," David said and reached for Lisbeth's hand. Holding it, he noticed her hand was ice cold.

"Well, what is it?" Ruth asked. She sprinkled salt on her mashed potatoes never taking her eyes off her son.

"Mom, Dad, I've asked Lisbeth to marry me," David said and smiled.

Ruth looked like she had been hit by an eighteen-wheeler truck and struck mute. Mr. Pittman leaned back in his chair with a big grin on his face and said, "Well, welcome to the family, Lisbeth. This is wonderful. Did my son get you a ring? That's what he's supposed to do."

Ruth was still in shock and mumbled, "My God, Lord Jesus! A ring?"

David tried not to roll his eyes, and told his mother, "We're going down tomorrow – to Tiffany's." He turned and smiled at Lisbeth. She smiled back and squeezed his hand.

"That's the way to do it, son," Mr. Pittman said with a broad smile. "Tiffany's, yes."

"David, you're rushing things. I don't see why you have to go to Tiffany's... We don't know who this woman is..."

"Mom, you need to be quiet. I love you but you're out of line," said David. "All you need to know is this. Lisbeth is the woman I want to have kids with and spend the rest of my life with. She said yes and I'm the happiest man on the planet. I'd love it if we could all get along. Mom, you need to stop acting like I've never told you or Dad anything about Lisbeth."

"I don't know, David. I just don't know," Ruth said. "I didn't know you were this serious about her." Turning to Lisbeth, Ruth asked, "Are your parents going to be able to pay for a real wedding? I don't want my son running off to some Justice of the Peace."

The doorbell rang and jerked Lisbeth back to the here and now. David stopped loading the dishwasher, kissed his wife on the cheek again, reassured her, and then walked to the front door. Within the next fifteen minutes everyone had arrived except Bob. Those who were there found a place to sit in the living room. David reached for his cell phone and called Bob

"Hey! Where the hell are you?" David asked. "What?" Seeing the frown on David's face, Kevin took the phone from his brother.

"Bob? This is Kevin. Don't make me come after you. Who? Yeah…well you oughtta be here in the next twenty minutes at the most. What do you mean? Put the driver on the phone." There was silence for a good two minutes. Kevin's eyes narrowed and he began to shake his head. He took a deep breath and let it out before saying anything. "Riverdale. Yes, Fieldston Road… Yes, I'm sure!"

David snatched the phone back from Kevin, "Look, sir, I don't know what your problem is. We know where we live. No, he's not lying. What's your name? Say what? Listen, I'm a lawyer, do you understand that? I'll be expecting you in the next ten minutes if not sooner. Yeah – well that's obvious. Thank you."

David turned around and found everybody looking at him. Catherine said, "Let me guess. He didn't think our kind of people lived up here and he was sure Bob was confused or maybe a thief, a well-dressed thief, but nevertheless a thief. "

"It's better than that. The jackass had already driven by the house and decided Bob had to be mistaken! Bob mystifies me sometimes," David said.

"The government ought to pay us for being Black in America," muttered Kevin. "You have to go through this shit every day, and then they wonder why we've got high blood pressure and get strokes."

"I hear ya'," David said and rubbed his brother on the back to give him some comfort. "It's the grammar of oppression and the punctuation of hate. Every damned day. You watch, the minute white people have to start living with the same uncertainty and stress we have to put up with their longevity rates are going to start dropping fast." He paused. David's eyes went blank, expressionless and he said, more to himself than anybody else, "And you have to raise children in this mess and hope to God…" David stopped. "And white folks wonder why black folks are so religious. It's the only thing we've got, because they can take all of this away from us in a New York minute," he said while motioning with his arm to the living room and the house.

Ruth walked to the kitchen and whispered, "Lord, how long? How long?" She looked out the window, not one leaf on any tree. The garden? Put to bed for winter. David stood in the kitchen door and watched his mother. She wiped a tear from her eye and tried not to cry. She straightened her shoulders, turned, and saw her son. "I'm getting old, David. And I'm tired." She walked back to the living room. "We need to talk later."

Catherine sat in silence. Kevin stood ramrod straight, staring into nothingness.

CHAPTER TWENTY
Victoria's Future

Bob arrived, haggard and angry. The skin on his face sagged. He avoided looking at Kevin. Bob was drowning in conflict. Everyone gathered in the living room. Lisbeth had made a fresh pot of coffee and a variety of sandwich sliders arranged on a tray she placed on the coffee table. Catherine tried not to glare at Bob, but it didn't work. Every time she looked at him, she flashed back to that night when she and their children saw him in bed with that young, white woman. Catherine remembered every insult, and every time his fist had hit her body when she was pregnant with Victoria. Ruth didn't bother to hide her disdain for him. Her face was a map of contempt. Every line on her face pointed to Bob's demise, at least that's what Ruth wanted. She didn't care if it was a sin. She wondered why he had to be there at all. As far as Ruth was concerned Bob was swamp scum on a good day! The fact that he was an educated man made it worse for Ruth.

Shifting in his chair, Bob cleared his throat and said, "I want to go on the record and say I'm opposed to letting my daughter go to some strange school. We don't know a damned thing about this school or that Solomon guy. I don't like it."

"Since when did she become your daughter? The daughter you couldn't take to her school's father-daughter dance," Catherine spit out.

"Whoa," David said! "Let's not rev up into madness."

Now Ruth and Catherine were glaring at Bob. Kevin, seated opposite of him, showed no emotion, but both hands were clenched into fists, opening and closing, waiting to serve and protect.

Lisbeth stood off to the side, leaning against the living room bookcase, wondering how she ended up in this family! She loved David and the life they created for themselves and their children, but his family… They were an intense bunch, she thought, and too damned smart for their own good sometimes, but they had no choice. Lisbeth's parents had also pounded into their children that familiar phrase one heard in so many black homes, "You've gotta be twice as smart to get half as much here." The implications and ugly truths behind that made Lisbeth tired and angry. Her father worked two jobs to make ends meet and her mother was a Nurse's Aide at Bellevue Hospital. Lisbeth had two younger sisters but they weren't anything like Victoria, the little brainiac! Lisbeth was convinced Victoria was an old soul just because of the calm, pensive way she often watched people. She had this unnerving way of flipping back and forth from an old soul to a twelve-year old child. Lisbeth couldn't imagine Victoria being any smarter than she already was, and shuddered thinking about what this little girl would face as she grew up.

David leaned forward in his chair and said, "Catherine asked me to look into this school given it's somewhere in the DC area, and I've got connections there…"

Catherine interrupted him. "David, let's cut to the chase. I asked some people I know at MSNBC to see if they could find anything – nothing. There's a website but if you want to get beyond the home page, you need a password. There's a phone number but you have to have another password or some kind of code before you can get connected to anyone! And Charles Solomon has an interesting connection given it's named, The Solomon School. What the hell is going on? And why didn't you want me to say anything at Sid's earlier this week? What is that?"

Frowning, Ruth whispered to her daughter, "You don't need to start cursing…"

Catherine looked at her mother wide-eyed. "Mom, are you serious?! Please."

"I didn't want you to say anything that would give them the impression you weren't going to cooperate," David said. "That would've made you vulnerable in their judgment and you would be considered a problem. Too dangerous."

"But what made you think Sid's place was wired? How could they do that?" Catherine asked.

"I didn't think anything. I had good reason to believe that based on what a friend told me, and I'd rather be safe than sorry." Catherine fell back into the couch, shaking her head.

"David, what did you find out?" Kevin asked. He kept one eye on Bob.

"My best advice, Catherine, to you and Bob, is let Victoria attend when she finishes at the East Side School or whenever Solomon wants her. Everyone who's been invited to attend The Solomon School has accepted. The kids who go there will end up running the world in twenty years if not sooner. The school is becoming one of the most elite, progressive academic institutions on the planet. Their students come from all over the world, all colors, all religions, all genders! Everywhere and everything and there's a counterpart for boys. I don't know where it's located and I wasn't told but I think it's in the Berkshires."

Catherine closed her eyes for a second before speaking. "We're already in over our heads, aren't we? Is it safe to talk here? I mean…"

David looked at his sister and nodded. "It's safe. I passed their test."

"What did I miss?" Bob asked. "What's going on?" He started to bite his lower lip while he looked at everyone. "C'mon, what am I not getting?"

David and Catherine told the rest of the family about the surveillance a few nights ago. Everybody was quiet.

"Are you saying Victoria is in danger?" Bob asked. "Is she going to be kidnapped?"

"No, just the opposite. In Solomon's mind, it's a done deal. Victoria will attend his school. Therefore, she has become absolutely precious to him and the world. He's going to make sure nothing happens to her. The people who were watching Sidney's place and following Sid and the kids, they were there for Victoria. Understand this, Solomon is concerned about Victoria's physical safety and emotional health as well. Do you understand?"

Catherine groaned and stood. "Lisbeth, where do you keep the wine?"

"Hey, hey," Kevin said to get his sister's attention. "You don't need any wine. It's going to be okay. Sis come on…"

"This is what's happened," Bob said with a sneer. "Her mother has become a drunk!"

Kevin extended his arm and pointed at Bob. "One more word… You understand?"

"Oh my God," exclaimed Ruth! "Let's just try to keep it civil. Can we do that Bob? Please."

"Okay," Catherine said. "Cancel the wine. David, how

much is all this going to cost? I know what Solomon said in the office, but there's got to be a catch. Nothing's free."

"Oh, there's a catch. You lose Victoria," David said. "And any obstacle or threat to Victoria's progress will be removed. You need to let that sink in. Charles Solomon always gets what he wants."

"He's not getting my daughter! Who the hell does he think he is? There're plenty of good schools here. She doesn't need his school," Bob said.

"Obviously, you don't get it. Listen carefully. Anyone standing in the way of Victoria's progress will be removed – permanently," David said. "Understand what I'm saying? He already sees you as a problem, Bob."

"How do you know so damned much?" Bob asked.

Ruth winced and turned away from Bob like he was phlegm someone had coughed up and spit on the sidewalk.

David gave Bob a look of hopelessness. "Bob, you don't handle the kind of cases I handle in DC for almost twenty years and not develop connections. You mention Charles Solomon and two things happen. You either get shut down with a polite but firm warning, or information flows to you. If it flows to you it's because he wants you to know. I got a call and was invited to lunch with this person I can't name, but he had top security clearance. I was told everything I needed to know because they wanted me to convey this to you. It's that simple."

Bob looked at David and raised his eyebrows. "Okay, if you say so... But let me ask this, who are these children? These children aren't normal. Something different, way different."

"You have been so cruel to Victoria. And now you're

demonstrating all this concern. Why?" Catherine asked.

"She's not my child. I know that."

"Bob, you're not making any sense," Catherine said.

"What are you talking about?" Ruth exclaimed. "You better say something! What do you mean, she's not your child?"

Bob threw his hands up in surrender and shook his head. "Never mind." Silence took center stage for almost a minute.

"David, what if Victoria doesn't want to go?" Catherine asked.

David got up and stretched before continuing. "Catherine, that's not likely to happen. He's already been flying up here working with her for at least a year if not more. I'll bet you dollars to donuts she's already become attached to him – and with Stephan gone. C'mon Cath. Connect the dots – or better yet, ask Victoria about him. Her eyes will light up! That cute little face will erupt into a smile. The fact that she hasn't said a word to you about their meetings until now makes her even more valuable to him. He's already had a chance to evaluate her. The only person she got that excited about was Stephan. Stephan and Solomon are her heroes. "

Ruth reached for a cup of coffee while mumbling, "Is there any conversation we can have without mentioning Stephan? You'd think he was part of this family. Lord... But David, why is Victoria so valuable to this Solomon man?"

"Mom, she can keep a secret, a grown-up secret at twelve..." David said. "Victoria has some unusual abilities, not all of them academic."

Ruth gave her son a knowing look and said, "There's a whole lot we don't know about Victoria."

"Ms. Butterfield told us almost two years ago she was outgrowing what they could offer... What do we do?" Catherine asked and looked at her mother.

"Sign the papers. Let her go and love her as much as you can between now and when she leaves," David said. "Money is not an issue at this school. Parents pay nothing. Tuition, room and board, books, supplies, travel…You won't have to worry about a thing. I'm sure it'll all be there in the contract. You'll have to sign something."

"I'm not signing," Bob said. "I don't like it."

"Then you'll be removed, Bob, one way or another," David said. He let out a big sigh and seemed resigned to something he wasn't articulating. "Look, let's eat this food Lisbeth fixed."

CHAPTER TWENTY-ONE
Everybody's Got a Role to Play

Bob left the Stockards, promising them he was going to fight this. He didn't want Victoria going to some swanky school somewhere near or in DC. For some misguided reason, he felt he could fight Solomon and win. He was going to find a way to talk with his daughter, convince her that The Solomon School is a bad idea. He convinced himself of this as he was being driven back into Manhattan. All he needed was an hour with Victoria.

Sitting in her son's living room, Ruth announced that she wanted to talk to everybody since all her children were there.

"What's wrong, Mom?" David asked.

"No, there's nothing wrong. Y'all c'mon now… Where's Kevin?" she asked.

"I think he's in the kitchen," Catherine said. "I'll go get him."

David leaned back in his chair and studied his mother for a moment. Whenever her speech slid back to that southern dialect, whenever the words y'all, c'mon, and fixin' marched out of her mouth David knew to expect something serious. Kevin and Catherine walked back in. Ruth looked around and asked for Lisbeth.

"Mom, you're sure?" David asked, really worried now.

"I'm sure," Ruth said. "Go get her."

David called for Lisbeth and within a minute or two she joined everyone in the living room.

Ruth looked at each one of them before starting. "Listen,

I've made a decision. I've been talking with your Aunt Clara. She's down there in that big house she and Jason lived in. Now that your Uncle Jason's gone, the house is too much for her. Your cousins are scattered, living in Chicago, Pennsylvania, and Los Angeles. I need to go back home. Clara's going to sell her place and move in with me back home."

"What?" exclaimed David. "Mom, look…"

She cut him off, "David be quiet and let me finish. I can't cope with all this anymore."

"All what, Mom?" Catherine asked.

"The world. I realized that when Kevin told me he was gay. I taught school up here for almost thirty years. We've got LGBT kids, hygiene classes now have to talk about birth control and sex, abstinence, drugs. We've got children from around the world who believe all kinds of things. Kids shooting each other in some of these schools. The police shooting kids… The girls dressin' half naked… And now, I've got a granddaughter who's smart in ways I don't even understand. I want to go home where I understand things."

"Mom…"

"David, please. I couldn't be prouder of all of you if I tried. Your Daddy and I worked hard to raise you so you would get a good education and be decent, God-fearing people. Kevin… it doesn't matter whether you're gay or straight. I'll learn eventually to accept it because you're my son. You're my baby and I love you. But it's time for me to go home. I don't want to die up here. I want to be closer to your Daddy anyway. He made me promise to bury him down home and when my time comes, I'm going to be right there next to him."

"Mom, don't believe all this nonsense about the new South. Them rednecks are still there, madder than ever because we had a Black President. Now they've elected a lunatic who's hoodwinked every last one of them. But they feel empowered now. We'd worry all the time," David said.

"David Stockard, I didn't raise no stupid children! Everyone in this room knows northern rednecks also exist. Wherever we go in this country, north, south, east, west... it is not safe for us and never has been. I'm beginning to think it never will be. At least I understand what's going on down home. I've had enough. Last week I called a realtor. She's going to come to the house next Thursday, take a look and let me know what she thinks it will sell for. I have to decide what I want remodeled down home. I know the kitchen needs work."

Catherine looked at her mother before speaking. "Is there anything we can do to talk you out of this? You can be a royal pain but we still need you, Mom."

Her brothers smiled and agreed.

"No baby. Nothing. Hopefully by this coming spring, I'll be gone. Y'all will do very well without me! You think I don't know that? Poor Lisbeth... I've been so hard on her."

Lisbeth walked over to Ruth and gave her a hug. "Ruth, I'm pretty tough. Don't worry about me."

"The one I'm worried about Catherine, is you, and that fool you married. You need to get on with that divorce. That man is not well balanced! The way he's hurt you and Victoria and Christopher... No... he's nothing more than an educated fool and a dangerous one at that."

Kevin tried not to laugh but it didn't work. David rested his chin in his hand and smiled.

"Mom, don't worry about Catherine and her kids. We'll watch over her," David said. "If you want to go back home, we understand. Go with our blessings and when you need us, we'll be there, like always."

Ruth got up and hugged her oldest son, whispering, "Oh baby, Thank you."

Catherine wanted to scream.

Oh my God! Aunt Sidney invited Mr. Solomon to her country house and he said yes! Everybody's going to be there. I think Mr. Solomon knew Uncle Stephan. Just a feeling I get. All the grown-ups are very nervous except for Uncle David and Aunt Sidney. As usual, they're very cool. Aunt Sidney bought me a tweed jacket with suede elbow patches to wear over my navy blue guernsey sweater and white shirt. I have new jeans and red ballet flats to match my red glasses. Red is just the best color in the world! I have to take my boots too but I'm definitely wearing my red shoes once I get to Aunt Sidney's. Aunt Sidney says fashion counts.

I can't wait for Mr. Solomon to come! Gram doesn't like Mr. Solomon. She hasn't met him but already she doesn't like him. I don't understand that at all. The only thing Aunt Lisbeth can think about is will the boring cousins behave. I worry about the boring cousins. That's all they do is behave. That's what makes them so boring. How do you ever learn anything if you don't break some rules? I wish they'd go out somewhere so we can concentrate on what Mr. Solomon has to say. Christopher's really curious about him. He keeps asking me questions. Mom's trying to pretend everything's normal. It's not. She asked me what I wanted for Christmas. I told her I had what I wanted for Christmas, Mr. Solomon.

"Victoria! Come down here right now so I can braid your hair!"

God! Mom's yelling. When I go to Mr. Solomon's school, we're going to have to do something about my hair. Mom can't fly to Washington to braid my hair! I don't understand why I can't cut it and wear it like Aunt Sidney's. The point is, I'm definitely going to Mr. Solomon's school. I don't care who doesn't like it!

Victoria, Christopher, Catherine, Sidney, Bonwit, and Coco were standing on the sidewalk loading Sidney's SUV. Bags of food, Christmas presents, books and their overnight bags. They would be at the country house for almost two weeks.

"C'mon. Everybody in the car," Sidney said.

Bonwit and Coco jumped in the back seat where they usually sat. Christopher and Victoria sat on either side of them while Catherine adjusted her seat belt. Sidney turned on the ignition and headed for the West Side Highway.

CHAPTER TWENTY-TWO
Solomon Meets the Family

They flew to the West Side Highway and up the Henry Hudson Parkway. Mr. Bunny and Misty the Owl were also in the back seat. Sidney turned on the radio as they slid north to the Hudson River Valley.

"Aunt Sidney! That's it! Turn it up! That's his song," Victoria screeched.

Startled, Sidney jumped a little, but she turned the radio up. She shot a quick glance to Catherine who shrugged her shoulders and rolled her eyes.

"Vic, whose song?" Sidney asked.

"Mr. Solomon," Christopher said. "Vic gave him a song. Listen. Listen to the lyrics."

In unison, Chris and Vic started singing, "Thunder and the lightening. Boom, boom, boom! Lightening and the thunder!"

"That's him, Aunt Sidney. Charles Solomon," Christopher said.

Catherine muttered to herself, "My God!"

"Chris, I didn't know you met him," Sidney said.

"Don't have to. If you listen to Vic…he's probably an earthquake too!"

The SUV rocked its way to the Taconic Parkway. At one point, everyone was talking and singing and barking at once.

Sidney pulled into the back driveway near the kitchen. Everyone jumped out, excited, giddy and impatient. Catherine was the last to get out. Bonwit and Coco ran to the back door and found Mazey, the housekeeper. She was an intense, dark haired woman with muscular arms who rarely smiled.

"Everybody inside," she said in a firm voice. "I'll finish. Go, go, go! It's cold. I made a fire. Come inside."

There was a lot of hustle and bustle. Victoria was close to exploding with excitement. Catherine immediately found some Chardonnay and strolled into the living room nursing a glass of white wine. She looked at the Christmas tree and started to tear up. She felt a hand on her shoulder. Turning, she found Sidney.

"Catherine, what's going on?"

"I don't know what the hell is going on anymore. I just don't. Did I tell you what Dr. Hudson asked me? About aliens?"

Bonwit and Coco started barking. "Cath, hold that thought. We have to finish this conversation." Sidney was gone in a flash. She ran to the kitchen looked out the window and saw a family size van pull in the back driveway. The Stockards, including Ruth, got out. David's hustling everybody inside. Ruth stood and looked around with an enigmatic expression on her face. The kids were teasing each other. Kevin waved his brother along indicating he would take care of their mother. David headed for the house.

Gleeful commotion filled the air as they took off their jackets and boots. Once done, the kids headed for the living room. It was filled with paintings, books, plants, photos of Sidney and Stephan. Max, Larry, Arianna and Geoff were a little intimidated by the surroundings. The tall, tastefully decorated Christmas tree presided over the room.

The adults hovered in the kitchen. And Victoria? Sitting

in a window seat waiting for Charles Solomon.

In between taking care of the last touches for dinner, all the adults were talking at once until Ruth said, "What do you mean Bob is coming? Why?"

"Speak of the devil," David said. "Here he comes."

"Why does everybody pull into the back?" Sidney asked rhetorically.

Mazey opened the back door for Bob and gave him a cold smile. "Mr. Pittman," she said. "I'll take your coat."

"Thank you," Bob said and handed Mazey his coat, scarf and hat.

"I'm going to put it here in the back hall closet. Everyone's in the kitchen. Can I get you anything?"

"No. No thank you." Bob surveyed the house. It made him feel less than. Was it the décor? The expensive art? The extraordinary craftsmanship? Or was it the presence of a man whose friendship Bob threw away? His heart pounded.

"Okay, you know where everything is," Mazey said.

Bob snapped out of it, nodded and headed to the kitchen. He walked in and everyone stopped talking. Catherine looked at him and walked away still nursing her glass of wine. David nodded and Kevin just stared.

"Bob, don't start anything while this man is here. Do you understand?" Ruth asked. "This is too important for Victoria."

Softly, Bob said, "I understand Ruth. I do."

"I hope so," she said. Ruth picked up her drink and "sashayed" to the living room.

"Bob, can I get you anything?" Sidney asked.

"No. Not now. I'm good."

Sidney gave him a look that made him slightly tremble.

"He's here! He's here," Victoria shouted. Like a missile she shot to the front door. "Uncle David! Uncle David, he's here. Where's Aunt Sidney?!"

Sidney and David joined Victoria as she grabbed their hands and pulled them to the front door.

"Take it easy, Victoria," David said.

"I am taking it easy!"

A limo glides into the front driveway and comes to a soft stop. Solomon gets out and looks around. Sidney's land consists of large, open fields along with acres and acres of woods and trails. Solomon surveys the sky, then notes where the fields are before walking to the front door.

By now, Victoria, David and Sidney were waiting for Solomon to ring the bell. Victoria couldn't stand still. The second the doorbell rings, Victoria opens it. She was beaming like a sunrise! Solomon greets Victoria first. He bends down, looks into her eyes and smiles. Sidney is captivated. David's curiosity is replaced by an unexpected sense of recognition. Charles Solomon is familiar to David. Victoria grabs Solomon's hand and stands next to him. She's exuding pride.

"Uncle David, Aunt Sidney, this is Mr. Solomon. I told you about him."

David extends his hand, "We've heard nothing but good things about you from Victoria. It's good to finally meet you."

Solomon shakes David's hand, smiles and says, "I'm thrilled to be here."

David has a look of amazement on his face after shaking hands with Solomon. David's puzzled.

Looking at Sidney, Solomon quietly says, "You are Sidney

Barrett Aldrich." They shake hands. Sidney is stunned and doesn't know why but she immediately warms up to him. "I'm thrilled to be here," Solomon says.

"Let's go meet everybody else," Victoria says. "They're in the living room." Bonwit and Coco were wagging their tales at him. Victoria pulls Solomon along and he looks at her adoringly.

The air is charged. It feels like tiny electric sparkles dance throughout the house. Mazey watches from the entrance to the living room. Sidney walks over to her.

"What's wrong with you, Sidney? You look like you've just seen a ghost or something," Mazey mutters.

"He feels like Stephan. That's all I know."

Mazey's face goes slack for a second and says, "I'm going to fix you some tea…with brandy." Mazey heads for the kitchen not understanding what was transpiring. All she knows is something different is about to happen. Unexpectedly, the house feels funny, like somebody else was there she couldn't see but feel.

Bob emerges from the back hall, sullen, with a frown on his face, hands in his pockets and eyes the reactions to Solomon.

Victoria introduces him to everyone. Kevin and David are watching from a corner. Kevin leans towards David and asks, "What the hell is going on?"

Ruth stares at Solomon, immediately smitten. He reminds Max, Larry and Geoff of a rock star. Arianna is trying not to gape. Her eyes are wide as dessert plates!

David snickers, pats his brother on the back, and says, "You gotta ask? You're witnessing the Solomon Effect. He wanted to meet Sidney. Asked for her."

"How does he even know Sid?"

"I know what he wants me to know. Nobody's giving up any information on this man. God knows I tried." David folds his arms across his chest and takes it all in.

Bob struts into the living room, chest puffed up, chin held up. He ignores Solomon. Seeing Victoria, he says, "Vic, come here and give your father a hug." He steps closer to her and Solomon.

"Get away from me!" Victoria says.

"Victoria! He's your father. What is wrong with you?" Ruth asks.

Christopher places himself between his father and Victoria. David and Kevin walk towards Bob. Ruth is alarmed. She stands to get ready, for anything. Solomon glares at Bob

"Everybody settle down. What's going on here? And don't tell me nothing." David turns and says, "Larry, Max, Arianna, Geoff, go for a walk. Do something! Now!"

The kids bolt. Victoria stands behind Solomon clutching his hand. Solomon's eyes scan each face with a rapidity and comprehension that's unearthly and paralyzing.

"Victoria, why don't you want your father near you? It's safe. Tell us, please," Sidney asked.

Victoria's eyes begin to blink in robotic fashion. It's what happens when she's on emotional overload and scared. Solomon bends down, looks at Victoria and says, "I won't let anything happen to you. Tell us the truth."

Ruth is amazed by Solomon's effect on Victoria and steps closer to get a better view of Solomon.

Victoria squeezes Solomon's hand. He squeezes back to reassure her. They look into each other's eyes. A few seconds later, she stops robotically blinking and looks at everyone. Solomon stands, places his hands on Victoria's shoulders and has her stand in front of him. He never takes his hands off her shoulders.

"Dad ties me up and throws me in the closet sometimes. Then he hits me and Mom pretends she doesn't know. That's when I get scared and can't do anything and I have to wait for Chris to find me and unlock the closet door. By then, Dad's gone."

Kevin lunges toward Bob, but Solomon stops him with one look. David and Christopher are breathing down Bob's neck, ready to grab him. Ruth's face is puffed with rage. Sidney stands like a witness getting ready to take an oath while sipping her tea and brandy.

"Let me have a word with Mr. Pittman," Solomon says.

"Oh c'mon. You're not going to believe Victoria, are you? Our little brainiac has a vivid imagination. She's just joking."

"No one's laughing here, Mr. Pittman. We should step outside." Solomon looks at Victoria and says, "You're going to be fine. Your Aunt Sidney and your uncles are right here. I'll be back in a minute."

Victoria nods her head and barely audible, says, "Okay. Please come back."

Solomon smiled, kissed her forehead and said, "I will. Everything's going to be fine." He looks at Bob and without saying a word, they leave the room.

Sidney looks around and realizes Catherine is gone. But Sidney's first priority is Victoria. Ruth watches all of this growing more and more alarmed and confused with each passing minute.

"Vic, let's go in the kitchen. I want you to help Mazey and

me finish dinner. C'mon." Sidney extends her hand. Victoria grabs it.

They leave the living room while David watches Solomon through the living room window. Solomon's back is all David can see. However, David can see Bob's face. It grows unnaturally still. Solomon puts one of his hands on each side of Bob's face and slowly lifts him. David quickly looks at Bob's feet. They were at least three feet off the ground. David's mouth opens slightly. Solomon lets go of Bob's face. As his feet touch the ground, his knees buckle and he collapses. Solomon says something to Bob. Bob closes his eyes.

David is breathing heavily. He turns and looks for Victoria. Leaving the living room, David meets Kevin in the hallway. The brothers stare at each other for a second or two.

"What is it?" David asked.

"If Solomon doesn't take care of Bob, I will. You gotta hear what Vic said."

"I think Solomon... Bob's gone. Where's Vic?" David asked.

"Vic was in the kitchen with Sid and Mazey. I'll tell them to come back to the living room. C'mon." Kevin said as he and David walked down the hall towards the living room.

CHAPTER TWENTY-THREE
Victoria's Father

Victoria huddles next to Sidney on the couch. Ruth is on the other side of Victoria, shaking her head slightly. Her eyes are on fire. Catherine's leaning against the wall by the living room entrance, arms crossed, shoulders high. She's unable to look at her daughter.

David walks over to Victoria. He pushes some magazines to the side of the coffee-table and sits opposite of Victoria. He gives her a slow smile.

"Vic, baby look at me," David says. "I'd appreciate it if you could tell me what's going on. It would help us protect you from your father."

"Mr. Solomon's going to protect me."

"How do you know that?"

"He told me he would," Victoria whispers.

"When? Today, last week, last month? When did he tell you?"

"A long time ago. I was three. He sat on the edge of my bed and told me he would come just in time so Dad wouldn't kill me, and he did."

"Oh mercy," Ruth mutters.

"Don't worry about your father anymore..." David mumbles.

"Victoria?"

Everyone turns towards the sound of the voice. It's Solomon. He fills the living room entrance. Victoria races from Sidney and flies into Solomon's arms.

Whispering into his ear, Victoria asks, "Where's Dad?"

"Gone. You won't have to worry anymore."

All the adults are dumbfounded. Carrying Victoria, Solomon looks at everybody and asks, "Would it be okay, if Victoria and I took a walk before dinner, before it gets too dark? Maybe Christopher and his cousins would like to come with us?"

"Of course. I think they're in my studio. We'll find everybody." Sidney leads Solomon and Victoria to her studio. Catherine starts to follow them when Ruth grabs her arm.

"You're staying right here, Catherine. I mean, right here. We're going to Sidney's den."

David and Kevin exchange looks and follow their mother and sister. Once there, Kevin looks at his shoes. David can't take his eyes off of his mother and sister. Ruth firmly closes the door to the den.

In a voice that sends the fear of God through her adult children, Ruth orders Catherine to, "Sit down."

"Mom, I don't…"

"You don't what? Answer me, Catherine." Ruth pauses and repeats, "Sit down on this couch, right now."

Catherine makes her way to the couch and sits in the far corner thinking the distance will save her from her mother's wrath. Her brothers know they better not say a word.

Standing in front of her, Ruth says, "Now get up!"

"Mom, please…" Catherine doesn't move. "I just can't."

Ruth reaches down and pulls Catherine to her feet, then slaps her. Catherine winces and tears pop from her eyes.

"Don't you dare cry! If I could slap the black off you, I would. Now you stand up straight and look at me… Now!"

Catherine tries to stand straight. She avoids looking at her brothers. This was too much like her adolescence where

Ruth always caught her doing something she wasn't supposed to be doing. Too often, her father came to the rescue, but he was dead now.

"I didn't raise you to endanger your children, to ignore their needs so you can keep a man. I wanted you to be happy, get married to a decent man, have some children and raise them so you'd be proud of them and they'd be proud of you. What in the world have you been thinking? What has this man been doing to my granddaughter?!"

"Mom, you don't understand. Victoria…"

"Don't open your mouth again until I'm finished. Not a word." Ruth steps back from her daughter, simmering with rage. "Your father is no longer here to bail your ass out of the messes you've made over the years. You worshipped the ground he walked on, but the one thing he asked you to do, you didn't. Matthew begged you not to marry that fool. Bob Pittman has done nothing but bring you misery. How can you be so damned smart and so stupid at the same time?"

Catherine sinks back into the couch. All her strength seeps out of her.

"No, no! Don't you sit down. Don't even look like you're going to collapse! Stand up!"

Catherine jumps up, wipes her eyes and looks at her mother.

"Don't you dare cry. You're going to sign whatever paper has to be signed and let Victoria go to that man's school. I can sense this is an extraordinary opportunity for her. When it's all said and done, no matter how smart that little girl is, she's still a black child in America. She needs every advantage." Ruth rubs her forehead before going on. "I've seen Victoria do things… And you have too. Don't you dare deny it. I've watched her read Pride & Prejudice in one afternoon! She's told me things that have come true. I've watched her bring dying plants back to life. Open your eyes, Catherine."

Catherine struggles to keep her composure. David and Kevin eye what's going on, growing restless with concern.

"It's the twenty-first century. I taught school up here for thirty to forty some years. These kids today have skills and thoughts and dreams I can't begin to understand and honestly don't want to. Things that shatter every belief I've ever had. I'm no fool. Solomon can teach Victoria things we can't even conceive of, and you know it. Whatever has to be done, do it! Get your behind down to Sidney's powder room. And don't think I don't know about your drinking. Go wash your face and act like you've got some sense for as long as Charles Solomon is here." Ruth looks at her sons and says, "You need to help your sister." Ruth leaves the den like a slow stream of hot, red-orange lava oozing from a volcano, leaving emotional devastation and destruction behind her that's not likely to be repaired.

Kevin and David try to console their sister. She waves them away and heads down the hall to the powder room when a wave of noise rushes in through the front door. All the kids, Solomon and Victoria walk in. Victoria's face is red from the cold, but her eyes are bright and there's a smile on her face. Dinner's ready for everyone.

CHAPTER TWENTY-FOUR
After Dinner

Solomon, Sidney and Victoria lead everyone from the dining room to the living room. They sit in front of a glass wall of windows, laughing and talking. Solomon keeps pointing to the night sky. Victoria is wide eyed. Sidney leans back in her chair and watches Solomon. For the first time in months and months, Sidney is relaxed. She feels content, completely comfortable and comforted by Solomon's presence. It scares her a little. She doesn't know why.

The cousins are getting more dessert before entering the living room like a platoon of soldiers. Kevin pours himself another glass of wine, while he fixes a cup of coffee for his sister. Catherine is desperate for a drink, a glass of wine, an aperitif – anything alcoholic. Short of that, Catherine wonders if Sidney has any chocolate, maybe some bon-bons with Grand Marnier in the center. Something! Kevin hands Catherine a cup of coffee with two teaspoons of sugar. She asks for a third teaspoon.

Ruth is laughing and talking with Mazey while rinsing the dishes before putting them in the dishwasher. Bonwit and Coco are watching for any cake crumps that might fall to the floor.

David whispers to his wife, "Let's go outside and get some air."

Lisbeth smiles. "Sure."

David tells everyone, "We'll be back. Gonna get some air. Behave, all of you. Remember, your grandmother is in the kitchen!"

Lisbeth giggles and asks quietly, "Was that supposed to

be a warning?"

"You know it! C'mon."

The sky looks like navy blue velvet sprinkled with twinkling diamonds.

Bundled up, Lisbeth says, "Dinner was good."

"Um-hmm. Sidney's a good cook."

"What's bothering you David? Ever since you and Kevin confronted Bob, got him out of the condo, you've had some nightmares. Talk to me. Please."

"Okay..."

Lisbeth and David lean against the stone fence that encloses the patio. They look through the wall of glass that encloses the living room. They can see everybody.

"David..."

"You know the only thing that made sense this evening was the food." He pauses. "Did you listen to what Solomon was talking about?" David turns and looks at his wife. "He talks about how mathematics is a galactic language, the connection between music and math... All his comments about how the human species is evolving - but we don't have enough wisdom. The kids were awe struck. And then there was Sidney..."

"What about Sidney?"

"I haven't seen her look that comfortable or interested in any man since Stephan died. Solomon made her laugh tonight, a lot."

Lisbeth grabs her husband's hand and says, "David, don't make me drag it out of you. What is it?"

"Don't laugh!" He squeezes her hand as a shooting star zips by. There's a small white light hovering in the sky that catches David's eye also.

"I know this is serious. I won't laugh."

There's a long pause before David says anything. "I don't think Solomon is human."

Lisbeth catches herself and swallows her scream. "What? What are you talking about? He's not human, then what is he?"

"Have you noticed his eyes? Just like Victoria's and Sidney's. They turn, become flat...got something to do with what he's feeling." David looks up to the sky for a minute before continuing. "Lisbeth, I watched him talk to Bob when they were outside. Sweetheart, Solomon's hands were holding Bob's face and Solomon lifted Bob off the ground. Each hand was on each side of Bob's face and somehow Solomon lifted Bob off his feet. What kind of strength is that?"

Lisbeth controls herself. She couldn't let the screams that were lining up in her throat out. She focuses on David.

"He let me shake his hand. It looked human but it didn't feel that way, and he wanted me to know that."

"What did his hand feel like?"

"Like steel, or chrome, or something damned close. He wanted me to feel that strength. The only other hand he's touched or held was Victoria's. God knows what Bob felt."

Lisbeth starts shaking her hands seemingly to keep them warm. She really doesn't know what to say. "Jesus, David! We're a successful black family in America. Nothing short of a miracle, and you're telling me that with all we have to contend with, now we've got to find room for Aliens?"

"I know how it sounds, Babe. I do. I really do."

"Hands Up, Don't Shoot! White supremacists! The KKK! Driving while black; these sick fools sending black coworkers emails with nooses, carrying the legacy of slavery every day and maybe twice on Sundays! The police are shooting Black people like we're animals! So now, just in case we get lulled into some false sense of security, we've got make room for Aliens from outer space!"

"That's exactly what I'm telling you! Babe, like the man said, "life ain't no crystal staircase." Bob looks up in the sky and sees that same small white light.

"I don't know... But whatever he is there's something sexy about him."

David turns and stares at his wife, amazed! "He's sexy? How sexy?"

"You don't have anything to worry about."

"You sure? 'Cause I can show you how sexy I can be right now! Right here on this patio."

Lisbeth laughs and grabs David's hand for dear life. He kisses and hugs her. Sighs heavily and still holding her, he says, "Solomon's come for Victoria like it was predestined. There's some deep connection Victoria has with Solomon and Sidney. I feel that whenever they're around. I can't shake it."

"What the hell are we talking about? C'mon! There's got to be another explanation. Aliens?! This is impossible," Lisbeth says and sits on the stone fence.

"Impossible? Heart transplants were impossible. Going to the moon was impossible. A black President was impossible. Us living on Fieldston Road and sending our kids to private schools was impossible. You want me to believe Solomon is impossible? Based on what? The limits of our imagination? I think the limits of our imagination are about to be blown sky high."

Lisbeth waits for a minute. "Is that it? That's what's been bothering you? Solomon's not human."

"No Babe, but Solomon and Sidney look like they're coming out here. Victoria's getting dressed too."

Lisbeth grabs David by the shoulders. "I know there's something else. I need you to tell me right now. Whatever it is, it's eating you up in some strange way. I want to know. Let me help you!"

David points to the window, watching Sidney, Solomon, Victoria and Catherine leave. "They're going to be here in a minute, Babe."

"David, damnit! Tell me."

"I think I was abducted," he says.

Lisbeth's face folds in confusion. "Abducted by who?"

"Aliens."

CHAPTER TWENTY-FIVE
Under The Night Sky

Sidney, Victoria, Solomon, David, Lisbeth, and Catherine gather on the patio. Kevin looks at them through the window and indicates he's staying inside. David nods his head in acknowledgement.

"Why are we out here? I mean it's cold," Catherine says.

"Sssshhh! Stop whining, Mom," Victoria whispers back.

"Where's everybody else?" David asks.

"They're wienies! They said it was too cold. They're stuffing their faces with popcorn, Uncle David," Victoria states.

Lisbeth tries not to laugh, as did Sidney and Solomon. It is cold but the sky was so clear and there were so many stars it was worth being cold. Lisbeth finds herself becoming awestruck. The silence is smothering.

"Follow me," Solomon says. Victoria runs and grabs his hand and Sidney's with the other.

David nudges Lisbeth and nods to walk toward them as Catherine reluctantly follows.

"You know, there's intelligent life out there. You have no idea," Solomon says.

"It is cold out here. Maybe I should go back to the house," Lisbeth said.

"Please stay. It's important that you stay," Solomon says.

Victoria turns, looks at her aunt and pleads, "Aunt Lisbeth, don't. Please stay."

"Okay, for you I'll stay," Lisbeth says. Solomon resumes walking with everyone following.

"Mr. Solomon, did you study astrophysics? Just curious,"

David says.

"David, we all come from the stars. As some of your indigenous people say, 'It is the stars from which we come and the stars to which we return.' "

They walk in silence until they reach the middle of a large field.

"Sidney, I didn't realize how much land you have out here," Lisbeth says.

"Yeah, there's a lot of land," Sidney says almost shyly.

"You hear that?" Catherine asks.

"Hear what?" David responds.

Within the next minute or so, everybody hears it. Victoria's eyes grow wide with excitement. Sidney is unusually calm while Catherine and Lisbeth tightly hold onto each of David's arms. His eyes are darting around, trying to locate the buzz.

"Look at the light," Victoria squeals.

The light grows closer and larger. Its trajectory is aimed at the field.

"What kind of star is that?" Catherine asks, barely breathing already knowing the answer.

Quietly, David tells his sister (and Lisbeth), "That's no star."

"What are you saying David? How do you know?" Lisbeth asks.

"The perimeter is smooth. Look how it's moving, deliberate, right towards this field rapidly."

"But there're things sticking out from it," Catherine says.

"Could be something like spokes or antennas, I don't know, but the point is, it's circular and smooth and moving towards us," David says. The closer it comes you couldn't deny that this was a U.F.O. of some sort with intelligent life on board. "Holy shit," mutters David.

During this time, Victoria and Sidney are next to Solomon. He has one arm around each one. He turns and says to Catherine, Lisbeth and David, "You're about to meet my colleagues." They stare at Solomon, not knowing what to think much less say.

The vehicle silently lands roughly a hundred feet from everyone. It occupies two thirds of the field that was over four acres. Not a sound is made. You can't tell where the doors are or any opening for that matter. A seamless panel opens from left to right, revealing part of the interior. Everyone reluctantly follows Solomon. David notices the U.F.O. is hovering slightly above the ground. The only thing that touched the ground was a ramp that appeared from the door. They reach the ramp and stop several feet from it. Lisbeth's mouth is slightly parted. She doesn't know where to look first. David is slack jawed. Catherine is weak all over. An elder, bone colored alien, with a female presence and a somewhat wrinkly face, spindly arms and legs, carefully makes her way down the ramp. Catherine almost faints but somehow stops herself. She wants to scream, but Solomon stops it with one harsh look. She tries to grab Victoria but Solomon's hand stops her. His touch makes her want to scream but she can't. Something is stopping her.

Lisbeth freezes. She can't believe what she was seeing. David suppresses a desire to walk up to the elder alien like an old friend. He's baffled by that impulse.

The elder has big, black, curious eyes that spoke a language all its own. When she blinks her eyes, it's a very deliberate, thoughtful action. She looks at everyone with a slight smile. And then the telepathic communication begins.

"We've been waiting for you. Welcome home, Sidney. Welcome to all of you. We've anticipated this for some time. Please…"

Sidney's awe struck. She looks up at Solomon and he smiles.

"Please, follow me," the elder alien says.

"I'm not going. I'm not going." Catherine faints.

Three of the Grays walk over to Catherine, place their hands above her body. Catherine's body rises two feet off the ground. The Grays guide Catherine's body onto the ship. Victoria can barely contain her excitement. None of these beings frighten her. For Victoria, this is a reunion. Solomon is the last to board the ship. The ramp closes and they find themselves in a white circular hallway. There are railings on the hallway walls and the light is bright as daylight minus the glare. Everything sounds like fluffy slippers. The noise is cushioned, the language gentle, muted, reminding David of melodious clicking noises or the African language, Xosa. The Grays are leading Catherine to another room. Before he can object or say anything, the elder alien communicates with David. "She will be fine. We'll take good care of her."

David was startled by her presence in his mind.

"Yes, we can read your mind," she says before he could ask. She turns and says, "Follow me."

David can't take it all in fast enough. To his left, several doors were open revealing spaces that reminded him of a hospital examining room, shiny gray tables, odd instruments attached to the nearest walls along with instruments hanging directly above the exam table. As he continues to walk by, he sees a creature he had dreamed about, and it scares him. Lisbeth's voice snaps him back.

"David! What is this place?"

He reaches for her hand. "We won't be here long."

They walk past another room and see roughly a dozen people, humans, lined up in various states of undress, several were wearing pajamas, others in work clothes. They were all races, all ethnicities, young, old, male, female. It's hard to tell if they were awake or in some kind of trance.

Sidney is overwhelmed but not afraid. A female alien passes her and greets Sidney telepathically. She looks behind her and notices that David and Lisbeth are being taken to another area. Shuffling by Sidney were four blue aliens wearing what appears to be baggy blue overalls or jumpsuits. Their faces appeared "smushed." Their bodies comparatively plump or thick and their demeanor, burdened. Other rooms are shrouded in what looks like frosted glass. All Sidney can make out were rows and rows of clear rectangular containers filled with liquid. Sidney focuses on them. She wants to know what the containers hold. Slowly she realizes, the containers hold embryos, some human, some hybrid, some more alien than human and some more human than alien. The last realization sends a chill through her body. At that moment, Solomon speaks to Sidney.

"Sidney, in here please." He motions to an opened door.

Sidney realizes Victoria is trying to reassure her. Sidney doesn't know why she thought about that, other than the reassurance she feels through their holding hands. Solomon puts his arm around Sidney's shoulder. They walk in. The room is dark, circular. But the wall in front of them is filled with what appears to be small television screens. They're all blank. It reminds Sidney of a television director's booth. The three of them sit on a circular bench made from some kind of metal she didn't recognize. The minute they sit the bench adjusts to their bodies.

"I remember. I remember now," Sidney whispers. Victoria grins. Solomon nods his head and the elder alien looks into Sidney's eyes.

"You want me to stay here with Charles?" Sidney asks the elder.

"Excellent," Charles said out loud. "I was afraid you had forgotten how to communicate telepathically."

Victoria nods her head at the elder alien with enthusiasm that borders on glee! They leave and walk down the hall, holding hands like playmates.

Sidney looks at Solomon and says, "I remember."

"Tell me what you remember," Solomon says.

She looks at the blank screens for a moment, laughs gently and proceeds.

"I was driving up the Taconic Parkway and I kept thinking I really had to pay attention. I don't know why I was thinking that except that it was easy to get lost if you took the wrong exit and didn't know where you were going. The next thing I remembered was being on a two-lane back road in some wooded area. I pulled over. Got out."

"Why did you do that?"

"I don't know. I felt like I was being called by someone. So, I pulled over to the side of the road and walked into the woods. I had gone maybe fifty feet or so when a Gray stepped out from the woods and led me to an open area and there was this little ship, maybe it was a shuttle. I don't know. It looked small but when I got on board… it seemed, felt much bigger."

"Do you remember why they needed to see you?"

"Oh yes. They wanted to check my nose, my left nostril to be specific. They examined it. Scared me to death. And they wanted me to see this," Sidney said and pointed to the screens.

"And…."

"You probably know what I saw! Future devastation on this planet, environmental destruction, riots, food rotting in supermarkets, climate change resulting in exaggerated weather patterns, wide swings in the temperatures, blizzards, hurricanes and floods almost of Biblical proportions."

"Anything else?"

"Of course. This is a test isn't it? To see if I'm ready."

Solomon laughs. His laughter comforts Sidney. She couldn't explain it, but his laughter is familiar. He stares into space before saying anything else.

"Sidney, it's you and Victoria," Solomon says.

"What about us?" Sidney asks trying not to show any concern or misgivings.

"Don't worry. Come with me," Solomon says.

They walk quickly to one of the rooms with the containers of embryos. Solomon places his hand on the wall and a door slides open. The room is cool and humid.

Sidney looks into Solomon's eyes. He returns her gaze. "You are a special hybrid, Sidney. You've been given the ability to identify someone's true intent among other things. That's important. We were so pleased with the choice you made. Rarely do humans want to study our spiritual reality and work to make all spiritual reality a bridge that we share." Solomon looks carefully at Sidney before continuing. "We've been tracking you since birth."

"The nosebleeds?"

"Yes, in part. But something else happened to you and you made a very wise choice that we can speak of at another time. What you must know is about Victoria. Catherine was simply the host because you couldn't carry Victoria. Victoria, genetically, has three parents, you, Stephan and me."

"What?!"

"Yes, it's true. Many children have been and are being designed to help your planet save itself. It might not work. Some of us are afraid it's too late. But now is the time for you and me to watch over Victoria. She already loves you and knows at some level Catherine and Bob are not her parents in the deepest sense of the word. Your husband was a genius. We took some of his…you call it DNA…and implanted it in Victoria. She must never see an ordinary human doctor. It's unlikely she'll get sick, but…"

"And if she does?"

"Call me," Solomon says. "Victoria is our mission. Now we must step up. I will take care of everything else."

The elder alien walks in and conveys, "All of you must leave now. There've been reports of our landing."

Solomon exhales heavily. He stands, reaches for Sidney's hand, "It could get messy. Let's go."

"I have so many questions," Sidney says.

"When we get back, I will answer your questions."

"Quickly, just one?"

"Yes, of course," he said.

"Why do you remind me so much of Stephan?"

Solomon smiled. "It's because I carry his consciousness."

"What?!!"

"I'll explain later. We must go." They leave the room and standing in the hall is Victoria. She looks at them, glowing!

"Victoria, what is it?" Solomon asks.

"I know. I know who you are. I knew it all along. I just had a feeling. I did! I love you!"

Solomon picks her up. Kisses her on the cheek while Sidney rubs her arm. "We must go."

CHAPTER TWENTY-SIX
The Ride Home

Sidney opened the front door. Bonwit and Coco ran to greet her, barking with tails wagging. Christmas music was playing and young voices are heard laughing and talking. Christopher walks to the hall with a thousand questions.

"Where have you guys been?" Christopher asks. Victoria, giddy, skips into the kitchen. Christopher notices his mother. She looked awful, weak, scared.

Ruth comes out of the kitchen, wiping her hands on a dish towel. "Where in the world have you been? We were getting worried."

David slips by his mother with Lisbeth close behind. Kevin ambles out from the living room.

"We were gonna call the police if you guys were gone much longer," Christopher said. Max, Larry, Arianna and Geoff wandered out from the living room also.

"Everybody," Solomon said in a loud voice. "It was my fault. I got carried away. There was much to see tonight."

"I'm going to bed," Catherine mumbled. "Mr. Solomon, thank you for a memorable evening. I'm sure I'll be seeing you again."

"Of course. Glad you came with us," Solomon said while looking her in the eye. She slipped up the stairs avoiding her mother and Christopher.

"Did you guys see that bright light?!" Christopher looked at them waiting for a response.

"It could've been a meteor, Christopher," Solomon said. "With so much wide-open space out here..."

"I don't think so," Christopher said. "I think it was a

U.F.O."

Max looked at his cousin and said dismissively, "Yeah, right. Why would a U.F.O. be here? Nothing interesting here."

"Look everybody, kids. Get your things. We need to get home. It's going to take us a little over an hour." David looked at his kids, motioning them to get their coats.

"Dad, what's the rush? Tomorrow's Saturday."

"Max, your father said get ready. So, let's go," Lisbeth said.

Solomon looked around for Sidney. She was standing slightly behind him. She caught him off guard. "I'm right here," she said.

Solomon smiled and telepathically said, "I have to go. I know you have many questions, but we'll be spending more time together. I have to take care of a few things. I'll try to come back later."

Sidney understood every thought of his. She felt like someone or something made several adjustments to her. She knew intuitively, some abilities had been awakened, but she didn't know how.

Christopher was watching them. He walked over and said, "What's going on?"

Solomon turns and looks at Christopher for a moment and then says, "I'll tell you before the New Year."

"Yes sir," Christopher said.

"Aunt Sidney, could Mr. Solomon come for Christmas?" Victoria asked.

"Oh absolutely. But he may have plans. Do you?"

"Well… I was going to spend some time with Claire and her family. But I'm sure we could work something out."

Excited, Christopher said, "That would be great!"

The Stockard clan moves en masse to the back door. "Sid," yelled David! "We're leaving."

Sidney hurried to them. "Come back! You see it wasn't that long a ride up here. I expect you back here for Christmas."

"That was really slick the way you worked that out," David said. He laughed, but not at Sidney. "It wasn't that long... I feel like I've been to the moon and back. Thank you for...an amazing evening." They look at each other trying not to crack up over the truth of it having been an "amazing evening."

Everybody jammed into David and Lisbeth's van. David follows the GPS directions and sails south to New York City. There is silence and the kids keep looking at each other wondering what's going on.

Ruth finally breaks the silence. "David, what is wrong with y'all?"

"Mom, I just have a lot on my mind," David said, eyes fixed on the road. It wasn't unusual for a deer to dart out from the woods and cause an accident.

"Like what?" Ruth asks.

"Let it alone, Mom, please," David said.

Ruth directs her attention to Lisbeth. "Lisbeth, what happened?"

"I've got less to say than David."

"I just don't understand. Y'all went out there, looked at the stars with Mr. Solomon, and what did y'all see? There was a bright light shining for a few minutes. Did you see that?"

Two police cars fly by, sirens blasting and lights flashing. Lisbeth and David exchange looks. Everyone else is looking out the window as a third police car flies by.

Kevin, grateful to be in the last row, watches the police cars vanish in the distance and said, "I wonder what's going on?"

Lisbeth closes her eyes, shakes her head slowly and looks out the passenger window, praying that she sees nothing else tonight.

CHAPTER TWENTY-SEVEN
A Nightcap

It was cold. Christmas was days away. Bob walks in a bar that's been recently renovated for a new upscale, gentrified crowd that was moving into Harlem in what felt like droves. This place had been "his" bar for decades. Now, he had to readjust. He opened the door. The place was almost empty. A white couple was seated in a booth, drinking what looked like wine and finishing a sandwich. With the renovations came a new kitchen, a modified soul food menu, and a juke box playing everything from Billie Holiday, Lena Horne, Nina Simone, Roberta Flack to Justin Timberlake, Cold Play and Maroon Five! At the end of the bar, a white man, well dressed and very intense looking, sipped a beer and watched the late-night news. It was hard to make out his face. Harlem was changing.

Bob sat on a stool. The bartender came over and said, "Man, where you been?! It's good seeing you. Listen, before I forget, thank you for helping my mom with her taxes last year. I couldn't do anything! I can do arithmetic but deciphering all that nonsense on those forms? Not me. So, thank you, man. Appreciate it." He hands Bob his drink with pride. "I remembered! An Old Fashioned."

Bob smiled. He took a gulp of his drink, hoping the events earlier that evening at Sid's would be washed away. He looks at the bartender. Bob nods his head in approval. "It's good, man."

"So, tell me. What's it like to live large like the white man?"

"Man, it ain't all that. Marriage is down the toilet. My

kids hate me. Shoot...I just moved in a condo around the street."

"Hey – man, I'm sorry."

"Yeah. It happens." Bob sipped his drink. "It's the kids, you know. They're really smart in ways I never knew about. And my daughter, wow. She goes to the East Side School for Girls."

The bartender stared at Bob before speaking. "You're kidding."

"No, why? You've heard of it?" Bob asked.

"Yeah man. I overhear a lot of conversations in here. Some of these white people would sell their souls to get their kids in there."

Bob finished his drink and said, "Well, I gotta go." Bob pulled out some money and threw it on the counter.

"Don't be a stranger," the bartender said.

Bob nods his head and walks out. The man at the end of the bar stood, paid for his drink, nodded at the bartender, and walked out. It was Charles Solomon.

Bob runs up the steps to the brownstone. While unlocking the front door, he looks around before going in. There was nothing unusual. He walks in his second-floor condo, takes off his coat, turns on some lights and heads to the kitchen. Boxes were half unpacked. The new couch and two club chairs still had price tags. There was a media center that held a flat screen TV in the living room. The kitchen was in disarray, but quite functional.

He opened the refrigerator, takes out a loaf of bread, a jar of mayo and some cold cuts. He closes the refrigerator, turns around and finds Charles Solomon standing there as cool and composed as a glacier. Bob dropped the jar of mayo.

"How the hell did you get in here?" Bob asked.

"We have some things to discuss. I'll be in the living room while you tidy up."

"Forget tidying up! What the hell do you want?" Bob looked around for any sign, any clue that would tell him how Solomon got in. There was nothing. Bob walked into the living room and sat in one of his newly purchased club chairs. Solomon stood over him.

"You've endangered Victoria's life, more than once, abused your wife and neglected your son who is going to be a brilliant architect one day."

"So what? They're my family. I can do whatever I want with them." Bob was breathing heavily and beginning to feel claustrophobic. Solomon was invading his personal space.

"I won't let anything happen to Victoria or her brother. You've been right, Victoria is not your daughter, nor is she Catherine's daughter."

In shock, Bob carefully shifted in the club chair. He leaned back and gaped at Solomon. "What the hell are you talking about?"

"Sidney, Stephan and I are Victoria's parents."

"You're crazy. Three of you? Right. Damnit, I knew she wasn't mine. She's a freak." Bob started to snicker.

Solomon's stance completely changed. He looked like a man who never knew how to smile. His eyes focused on Bob. Solomon sat down opposite of Bob and said with detached intent, "You have to die. You have to leave this world. There's another place for you."

"I have to die. From what?! I'm perfectly healthy," Bob announced.

Solomon gave him a cold smile and stated, "You have

high blood pressure and you haven't been taking your medication." Solomon focuses on Bob's head. Bob grabs the side of his head and falls back in his chair. Solomon takes his pulse. No sign of life. He looks around the condo, searching for something he knew wasn't there, a photo of Victoria, anything that would indicate Bob had some affection for her, but there was nothing. Solomon sighs and leaves by walking through the wall.

CHAPTER TWENTY-EIGHT
Benedictine & Brandy

It was after midnight. Everyone had either gone home or gone to bed except for Sidney, Bonwit, and Coco. Most of the lights were off downstairs. One lamp was on in the living room where Sidney sat wrapped up in a blanket with her spaniels, sipping a cordial of B&B, Benedictine and Brandy. The fireplace held a soothing fire. The Christmas tree sparkled. This was the first time she had a chance to sort through everything that had happened earlier. In the background, Andrea Bocelli was singing, "Time to Leave." It was one of Stephan's favorite pieces of music and was played at his funeral. She could get lost in the meaning of it. A few tears slipped down her face. She took the edge of the blanket and wiped them away. Every day she asked, "Why did you have to leave, Steph? Why?"

There was a soft knock at the front door. The spaniels trotted to the door, tails wagging, but no barking. Still wrapped in her blanket, Sidney walked to the front door and stood there for a minute, watching her spaniels, and trusting their instincts. Nobody ever came to see her this late. She looked through the peephole and immediately opened the door.

Charles Solomon walks in. Bonwit and Coco's tails wag faster. They sniff his shoes. Bonwit jumps up and leans against him. That's exactly how Bonwit would greet Stephan.

Taking his jacket, Sidney asks, "Is there anything wrong. Did you forget something?"

"No. I came back to talk with you, privately. It's important."

"You should've stayed. Please, come in. Can I get you anything?" Sidney asked.

"No, I'm fine," he said. He carefully put his arm around her shoulder and they sat on the couch. The spaniels stretched out between them and the fireplace. Noting the blanket she had wrapped around her, he asked, "Have you always had trouble with the cold?"

Sidney smiled and said, "Yes. I won't ask how you know that."

"I want to thank you for watching over Victoria. You and Stephan had and still have an enormous impact on her life. We didn't anticipate the rage Robert Pittman developed."

"Who would've seen that change in his personality," Sidney said.

"Sidney, your world, this planet is changing. Some of us are very worried, not about the changes, some will be unavoidable, but how the human species will handle it."

"What do you mean? Like climate change?"

"Yes, that's a very large part of it. But the more significant changes have to do with human morals, generosity and the extraordinary greed and hate. Some of us who work in the light don't have much time to put things in place. We're not alone. There are many of us from different realms all over the universe."

Sidney was having difficulty forming a response to Solomon. She looked into the fireplace and asked, "Who else is here?"

"There are several races working with your government," Solomon said while watching for Sidney's reactions.

"Doing what? Do I dare ask?"

"Nothing good and there are other governments on your planet working with them also. Sidney, you know that saying, '…as it is above so it is below…" She nodded her head. "There's good and bad everywhere, below and above."

"Why is everything a secret?" Sidney asked.

"It won't be much longer." Solomon shifted his weight and looked at the fire.

"Charles, what do you want me to do?"

"Right now, help us raise Victoria. Protect her. All the qualities and abilities we designed for you will begin to blossom now instead of erratically appearing and leaving people dumbfounded. Claire Butterfield will help train you, refine your skills and be…someone who will watch over you and Victoria as well."

"I'm beginning to think there's something dangerous about to happen."

"Well, you're right. Your government is very interested in Victoria and several other students at my school. You should know there are people in your government who are working with us also. They see the possibilities for good," Solomon said.

"That's the way it always is, isn't it? Opposing sides, dark versus the light. Yes?"

Pensive, Solomon looked at the fire and said quietly, "Yes. Always."

CHAPTER TWENTY-NINE
A Loose End

Mazey was unloading the dishwasher while Sidney was sipping a cup of tea. Solomon didn't leave until 2 AM that morning. Staring into space she remembered their talk about the afterlife, Stephan's consciousness…

Solomon looked at her and said, "I don't want you to be afraid."

"Just tell me, please."

"You know there's no death?"

"I know Stephan's gone from this realm."

"Sort of." Solomon paused. "I'm going to leave you with this to consider. The afterlife is a range of vibrations. Some afterlife vibrations are very close to the vibration of my realm. There are some humans who are open to the afterlife vibration also, naturally."

"What does that mean?"

"It means that my realm has easy access to those in the afterlife. The truth is we all go to another life. It's no one place, Sidney. It's vast. There are some who arrive and find themselves in a world similar to here or where they came from. Others go to higher realms. The higher vibrations of the afterlife are magnificent, what some of your kind think of as angelic. Stephan loves you. That hasn't changed. What you need to know tonight is you can reach him, through me or through your own abilities. If you wish, I will show you how to reach him. You have the ability to do that if you want to. The two of you were meant to be and still are. The connection remains. We didn't count on him being murdered."

"I knew it," Sidney whispered.

He stared at Sidney for a moment. "It's like your radios here."

Sidney remembered just staring at him, unable to speak.

Solomon smiled. "Your radio stations, each station has a channel, a vibration. Each one of us has a vibration. The vibration that you and I have are very close to the vibration of the afterlife. That makes it easier for us to communicate and come in contact with the other side. It's easier for us to find the right channel. That's enough for tonight," Solomon said. "Stephan hasn't died. He's simply changed. All of us will change."

Trying to hold all that Solomon told her last night made Sidney very tired. The phone rang and jolted Sidney from her thoughts of last night's conversation with Solomon. She picked up the phone and could barely hold it.

"Hello?" she said. "Yes, she is but I'm afraid she's still asleep." There was a long pause while Sidney listened. "My God. Hold on please."

"What's wrong?" Mazey asked.

Sidney raced up the stairs with the phone, knocked on Catherine's door and went in. She shook Catherine, saying, "Wake up! Cath – c'mon, wake up."

Catherine opened her eyes. "What?"

"It's Brendan," Sidney said and gave her the phone.

Catherine takes the phone, sits up, and with a voice that sounded like it was wrapped in a sweater says, "Brendan? It's Catherine. What's going on?"

Sidney watches her. Catherine's eyes stretch open and her face becomes limp, expressionless. When finished, she hands the phone back to Sidney.

"Cath?" Sidney asked, her face wearing a stunned frown.

Catherine looked up at Sidney and said, "It's Bob. He's dead."

"What?!! What are you talking about?"

"He didn't show up for work, so Brendan sent somebody over and they found him. I've gotta get dressed, go down and do something, claim the body. What do I tell the kids? How are they going to take it? My God!"

"I'll drive you," Sidney said. She left Catherine and went into her bedroom to get dressed. Standing in her dressing room, she threw on some jeans, found a sweatshirt, and started looking for some shoes. Sidney selected a pair, grabbed some socks, went into her bedroom and found Victoria. "Hey, sweetie."

"He's dead, isn't he?" Victoria asked, her voice empty of any emotion.

Sidney thought for a moment and then simply answered, "Yes."

Victoria took a deep breath and then exhaled. "Good."

CHAPTER THIRTY
"…keep your faith strong…"

The Christmas holidays were in the past now. Bob's funeral was a small gathering of colleagues and a few friends from childhood. Catherine was numb. She wanted everything that reminded her of her life with Bob to be over. She found herself wishing that this incredible reality concerning Victoria, who may or may not be her daughter, with Christopher rapidly becoming a young man and also growing attached to Charles Solomon, and her being regarded by the family as a royal fuck-up, to be over also. The PhD didn't matter. Catherine had two things to hold onto, her work, and her friendship with Sidney, a friendship wrapped in contradictions, affection, and more than a little jealousy. Catherine couldn't imagine why she was needed for much of anything. She said to herself, "I can be easily replaced. Nothing special about me."

David, Catherine, Sidney, and Victoria were standing outside of Reagan International Airport waiting for a limousine that Solomon was sending to take them to the Solomon School for Girls.

Victoria was eagerly looking for the limo. She had a multi-colored knitted hat on, the collar of her coat pulled up and a navy blue scarf wrapped around the collar. The cold turned her cheeks ruddy red, like Sidney's, who was standing right behind her. A middle-aged woman rolling her suitcase along saw Sidney and Victoria. She stopped, a big smile on her face and said, "What a cute little girl you have! The resemblance is so strong."

Catherine closed her eyes and turned her face away.

Sidney smiled at the woman and said quietly, "Thank you." Victoria beamed.

David adjusted his fedora hat, and said to no one in particular, "I don't often fly by private plane. Wow… It was very nice. Solomon's sparing no expense."

Victoria started jumping up and down. "The limousine! It's coming! I see it!"

Everyone squinted. There were several limos pulling in and out. A dark, navy blue limo pulled up next to them. The driver briskly walked over. His smile was flawless. He was average height, but he looked so very perfect. His skin was smooth, without blemishes or stubble. David wasn't sure he shaved at all. And then, there were the eyes. David gave a sigh of resignation. The driver's eyes were just too damned dark.

"Another one," David thought. "How many of them are blending in with us? I'm beginning to think they're everywhere. Damn."

"This is the Stockard party, yes? Mr. Solomon sent me."

David responded, "That's us."

"Very good. I'll be your driver while you're here. Do you have any luggage?"

Catherine piped up and said, "No, this is a day trip."

The driver nods, opens the passenger door and everyone got in. They pulled out and headed to northern Virginia.

Victoria's face was a round bag of smiles, joy, and excitement. Catherine watched her and also smiled.

"I've lost my little girl," Catherine thought. "She's really Sidney's daughter. No wonder Vic took to Sid so soon and so deeply."

It was hard to comprehend. Every now and then, during

the past two months, Catherine considered signing herself into a mental hospital, someplace, any place where she could forget and somebody in a white coat would tell her none of this happened, that she was hallucinating, that she had a psychotic break with reality. Instead, her therapist gave her a book on abductions written by a Pulitzer Prize winner, a Harvard psychiatrist!

"Maybe I should track him down," Catherine thought. David's voice brought her back to the here and now.

"Sir, exactly where is The Solomon School?"

"Not very far, Mr. Stockard."

"But what does that mean? Ten minutes, an hour…"

"Sir, enjoy the ride. Traffic's moving and we'll be there in no time."

David smiled. He knew the driver would tell him only what Solomon wanted. "This is a tight operation," he muttered.

"What did you say?" Catherine asked.

"Nothing."

Holding Sidney's hand, Victoria looked at her uncle and said, "It's going to be fine, Uncle David."

"I know. I was just curious."

David looked at Catherine and Sidney, hoping he conveyed calm and confidence. After what felt like a half hour, the limo turns down a long road that was really the driveway leading to the Administrative Building. The Solomon School looked like a Gothic English Prep School. Additional limos were arriving with parents and accepted students. Victoria eagerly scans the campus. Her eyes miss nothing.

She turns to Sidney and says, "I don't think this is real."

Stunned, Sidney says, "What do you mean, Vic?"

"I don't know. But it's not real like we know real. But it'll be fine."

"Oh God… Victoria, I need a favor from you, okay?" Catherine asked. "I don't need to know what you're sensing. This place looks real to me. Just for while we're here, let me believe it's real."

Victoria looked at Catherine, puzzled, then looked at Sidney and back to Catherine. "There's no need to be scared."

"Okay," Catherine said barely audible.

The limo pulls in front of the entrance to the Administrative Building and stops. The driver pops out and opens the passenger door for everyone. Victoria can hardly wait. She hops out and sees her best friend from the East Side School for Girls and shouts, "Ginger!"

Ginger turns her head and Victoria runs over to her. Ginger is a model of sensitivity and perception. Just a little taller than Victoria, with the same dark eyes that Sidney and Victoria have. Ginger had olive skin, framed by straight, black, shoulder length hair. They hug and rock from side to side several times giggling.

"I'm so glad you're here," Victoria said.

"Me too," Ginger said. "I'm glad you're here. Maybe we'll be roommates."

A perky young woman walks out to greet everyone and leads them to the lobby. There were several chairs, a receptionist sat behind a very streamlined desk. Other parents and children milled about, taking in the sharp contrast between the Gothic exterior and the ultramodern, minimalist interior. Large, framed photos of the galaxy were displayed with explanations of exactly what one saw in the photos. Suddenly, everyone is silent.

Charles Solomon entered with two women following him, Ms. Tyler, Dean of Academic Studies, very lean and tall, with pronounced features, narrow, dark eyes, almost Asian in appearance, and Ms. Cohen, Dean of Student Life, petite with piercing eyes, shoulder length silver hair, and an air of mischievousness. She had blue-green eyes that sparkled from time to time. Ms. Cohen was oddly ageless.

"Welcome to the Solomon School for Girls. I'm delighted you could make it. Ms. Tyler and Ms. Cohen will give Victoria, Ginger and her parents a tour. I'd like Sidney and David to come with me. Catherine, please go with Ms. Tyler. In a moment, several guides will be out and escort the rest of you on a tour of the school, its facilities, and its grounds. We will all have a chance to talk before the day is over."

Victoria puffs up with excitement and she and Ginger are whisked away. Solomon takes Sidney and David to his office as Catherine watches them leave.

"Mrs. Pittman," said Ms. Tyler. Her voice resonated with a depth that unsettled Catherine. Jittery she caught up with Ms. Tyler. Catherine noticed that Victoria gave her an annoyed look.

"C'mon Mom," Victoria hissed! "We've got lots to see."

"Victoria, I'm coming," Catherine said and realized for a second Victoria was her superior, older and somehow wiser.

Solomon ushers Sidney and David into his office. David was immediately struck by the absence of windows in Solomon's office. It was sparse, a huge desk embedded with three computer screens, and an ergonomically shaped chair.

There were two additional chairs in front of his desk and behind Solomon was one of the largest photographs of some galaxy that David had ever seen. He was captivated by its clarity. It gave high-definition new meaning. There was nothing else. The tan, wooden walls were bare. David couldn't find the door they had just walked through.

"Please sit. Can I get something for you? Tea, coffee, maybe… a soda?"

Sidney and David declined and sat down in front of his desk. The minute he sat down David grew alarmed. Sidney showed no discomfort.

"Mr. Solomon, what's with the chair?"

He smiled and said, "The chair is molding itself to your body for maximum comfort. Anything else you notice?"

"I'm fascinated by the clarity of these photos you have. The one behind you looks like I could reach out and touch the stars. It's magnificent." David started to say something but changed his mind. He felt foolish but he would've sworn the room was breathing, that it was a living, organic thing. There was a foreboding quality about it that made David hypervigilant.

"I'd like to show you some of the additional areas of our school," Solomon said. "Please, come with me."

Sidney and David followed Solomon over to one of the blank walls in his office. Solomon put his left hand on the wall and a door opened, seemingly revealing an elevator, but it looked more like a large tube. They stepped in and as the door closed, Solomon quietly said to David, "That was not a photograph, Mr. Stockard." Solomon looks straight ahead smiling. Sidney wanted to laugh but she didn't. David decided he would stop thinking for the moment and just "go with the flow."

Given the length of time they stayed in this tubular elevator before it stopped, David was convinced they were higher than the main building that was four stories. David thought to himself, "We are way past four stories. What the hell is this?"

The elevator door opens and Sidney and David follow Solomon down a long, sparkling white hall that reminded them of the ship. David was preparing himself in case he saw any of those little gray beings slide down the hall, but there was nothing and no one. They reached what seemed like the end of the hall. Solomon placed his left hand on the wall and like before a door slid open. The entire back wall of the room was another "photo" of stars and clusters of stars. Sidney whispered to David, "We're no longer on earth."

David had no time to react, because in front of the window was a conference table. Seated were ten non-human yet humanoid Beings staring at them along with four members of the U.S. military, dressed in full uniform. Solomon walked to the head of the table and sat down, pointing to two empty chairs for David and Sidney.

Looking at David, Solomon said, "When the time comes, we will need allies on earth."

"When the time comes for what?" David asked trying to hide the exasperation and fear in his voice. His heart was racing. His chest was in pain and he hoped he wasn't having a heart attack. David glanced at Sidney, the picture of calmness. Now his head was pounding. He really wanted to scream. The beings sitting in front of him were the icing on the cake. David kept hearing his mother's voice telling him,

"Don't you dare cry."

"The transition, and it's already started. We must identify allies now. In return, all of your family will be kept safe. You may tell your wife, but not your children. It's for their own protection. They can't tell what they don't know," Solomon said.

David looks at Sidney and asks, "Did you know about this?"

Sidney dropped her head for a minute and returned David's wide-eyed gaze, "Yes," she said.

"All my colleagues here represent different planets and two different realms from another dimension." Solomon leans forward, looks David in the eye and says, "We've been walking among you from the very beginning, from the minute earth was created. We have a huge investment in this planet. It's in our best interests that earth not only survives but thrives. But there's only so far we can go. We cannot defy universal law."

"Where is our government in all this?" David asked.

"In the dark," Solomon stated, "except for a select few."

"Can you elaborate on that?" David asked trying not to stare at the beings who were staring at him.

"No. But we have to know before you leave this room if we can depend on you as an ally. I will be your contact, David, along with these members of the military."

A heavy-set man at the far end of the table in a US military uniform stood. "Mr. Stockard, my name is Colonel Theodore Petersen. We know a lot about you so you will understand what I'm about to say. Mr. Stockard, we have a situation and we're trying to rein it in before we run out of time. When the time comes, we will need your skills."

David glanced at Sidney and asked, "Are you an ally, also?"

Solomon said, "Sidney is family."

David took a deep breath, looked around, hoping there was an answer hanging magically in the air. "Are we really on the verge of destroying earth?"

"Yes, in multiple ways," Solomon said.

Colonel Petersen sat back down and said, "We're on the verge of ending this society. There's a lot wrong here, Mr. Stockard."

"Okay, okay. I'm in," David said, not knowing what he was agreeing to at all. "Keep my family safe. That's all I ask."

Solomon smiled and said, "Excellent. We are very pleased and of course we'll keep your family safe."

CHAPTER THIRTY-ONE
It's All about Victoria

Ms. Cohen and Victoria bounced down a hallway, lined with classrooms on either side. All were sparkling white with odd looking computers that were very, very thin. There was a large screen in the front of one room, no desks, no chairs, but cushions lined up in two half circles on the floor and four stacks of mysterious silver slabs.

Victoria pointed to some markings outside of each classroom, markings that resembled hieroglyphics. She looked at Ms. Cohen and said, "I know what that says."

Ms. Cohen smiled and said, "Yes, you remember. That's wonderful. We're so pleased."

"Where're we going?"

"To meet some students. I think you'll recognize some," Ms. Cohen said.

Victoria swelled with excitement. The wall curved and Ms. Cohen stopped. She placed her left hand on the wall and a door slid open revealing a big circular room with twelve hybrid children. Most of them appeared to be more alien than human, but there were five you couldn't distinguish from human children except for their dark eyes, that made one think of liquid pools of black ink.

The hybrid children turned to see who was coming in. Five of them ran over to Victoria, shouting her name.

"Victoria, you're back!"

"I know! I'm so glad to see you," she said. Victoria's face lit up with joy.

The teacher stepped forward, an alien, beige, youngish, welcoming eyes with a female presence. There was an air of calmness about her. She moved her thin body carefully and began a telepathic conversation with Victoria.

"Victoria, do you remember how to create?" the alien teacher asked. "Create objects?"

"I haven't been able to practice," Victoria said telepathically.

"But you have remembered how to communicate telepathically, haven't you?" the teacher asked. "Come, let's sit together with some of your friends and see what can happen."

Victoria sat with four other hybrid children in a small circle. They talked to each other for a few minutes and then held hands and focused on the center of the circle. Several minutes passed and then slowly a box began to form, seemingly out of thin air. The fact was, the electrical energy from the hybrid children's brains created the box. It was solid as a rock. Ms. Cohen looked at the teacher. They exchanged satisfied smiles.

"Very good," the alien teacher said.

"What happens to the box," Victoria asked.

"It's kept with the others. It will be examined and studied, and the results shared with the students. We can learn from it. We are so glad to have Sidney with you. Some of our students must learn how to play. Sidney has been helping. Now, you must go. We will see you soon."

Fifteen minutes later, everyone was in the lobby of the main building. The kids were giddy with excitement. The other parents? Quite sober from this new reality they'd seen. They talked in whispers if at all. Catherine, Sidney, Victoria, and David were waiting to be called when their limo arrived.

"Vic, what are you going to tell Christopher when we get home?" David asked. "He'll want to know."

"Mr. Solomon already talked with Christopher," Victoria said very matter-of-factly.

David looked at Catherine, then Sidney. Catherine shook her head. Sidney just closed her eyes. "How do you know, Vic?"

"Christopher told me."

Ms. Cohen walked over to them, touched Catherine's arm. "Catherine, Mr. Solomon would like to see you before you leave."

Catherine's face froze. "Why does he want to see me?"

"Mrs. Pittman, please."

"Mom," squealed Victoria. "Go!"

"Okay, I'll be right back," Catherine said. She followed Ms. Cohen to Solomon's office and was escorted in.

Standing to his full height and without a smile on his face, Solomon dismissed Ms. Cohen. "I would ask you to sit down, but this isn't going to take very long, although your limo will wait if we need more time."

Catherine's breath grew shallow and she wanted to run, but her legs felt like lead weights. She managed to say, "What can I help you with?"

"Are you beginning to understand the magnitude of all this?" Solomon asked.

"I think so," Catherine said.

"Your husband's gone because he endangered Victoria's life. Let me be very clear, I would hate for that to happen to you. Understand there are many ways to remove you. The only reason I'm hesitating is because of Victoria. She does love you, but she also loves Sidney, and Victoria would understand if you became sick and had to be permanently institutionalized or removed. Am I clear?"

"Absolutely, Mr. Solomon."

"Can we trust you?"

"Just give me a chance. I'm going to do everything I can."

"I hope so. Have a pleasant trip back to New York, Mrs. Pittman. I'll be coming out to say goodbye to Victoria."

The driver opened the passenger door for everyone. Victoria waved goodbye to Ginger, who was getting into another limo with her parents. Catherine and David got in. Solomon catches up with them and walks over to Sidney. He reaches for Victoria's hand and she grabs it.

Looking at Sidney, he said, "We'll see each other soon. We have a complicated path to walk."

Sidney smiles and touches his arm. He bends down and holds Victoria by the shoulders, smiles and telepathically tells her, "I love you. I am very proud to be a parent to you."

Victoria grins. "I promise I'll be good."

"You and Christopher stay with Sidney," Solomon says. He kisses her on the forehead.

"It's going to be a great adventure, isn't it?" Victoria asked.

"It will be amazing," Solomon says and Victoria hugs him before jumping back in the limo.

The driver pulls away. David looks out the back window. There's no trace of the Solomon School. It had vanished. David's head whips around and stares straight ahead. Catherine is watching her brother. Sidney and Victoria are talking and the driver catches David's eye.

"Not to worry sir. Everything's fine! Victoria has her

family and we'll take very good care of her." The limo slid along the country road and headed for the airport.

Drawings by Janis A. Pryor

Owl Photograph enhanced from Unsplash

- Screen memories are often recalled by Experiencers who have been abducted. A screen memory is a familiar image or object that can be tolerated and used unconsciously as a screen against a memory that would be distressing or shocking if remembered.

- Webster's New World College Dictionary, 4th Edition. Copyright © 2010 by Houghton Mifflin Harcourt. All rights reserved.

www.ingramcontent.com/pod-product-compliance
Lightning Source LLC
Chambersburg PA
CBHW070950190726
48292CB00004B/1405